Deadly Attraction

ANGUS BRODIE AND MIKAELA FORSYTHE MURDER MYSTERY
BOOK THIRTEEN

CARLA SIMPSON

Prologue

EARLY JUNE, 1893

THE CELLAR WAS cold and damp and smelled vaguely of mold and other sharper scents of paint, oil, and turpentine beneath the glow of electric lights at two stands that stood opposite each other.

She wanted desperately to sleep. But she already knew the consequences if she relaxed even a little to ease the ache in her back. Over and over again, and then ...

"Lift your chin!" came the icy command. "Now look at me! Yes, that is it.

"You're thoughtful ... now sad. Now, lower your gaze. Let me see exactly what you are feeling and thinking."

She did as she was told. It took no skill or great effort as the silk wrap slipped from her shoulders and exposed bare skin.

She shivered. Not so much from the cold, she was used to that from the early hours of the street market. It was from the anger in that voice, far colder, without any feeling.

"Now, smile softly. You have a secret, a lover perhaps. You can feel his warmth, the touch of his hand on your bare skin. What? No lover?"

That voice, teasing, taunting, then laughter, chilling very much like the room so very cold. She forced her thoughts away from that. She had hoped ...

But there was only that voice.

"Look at me! Imagine that your lover is here, watching you from the shadows. You cannot see him, but he sees you. You are shy, but there is also anticipation for something you have never known. Yes! That is what I am looking for!

"Do not move! Do not breathe! You must remain very still!"

She held herself as she had the past days, perfectly still in spite of the fear deep inside, hoping that each day was the last one—through countless sketches, the way she was touched, a hand moved, the silk cloth wrapped around her almost like a caress that made her shiver, exposing her.

There was no sleep, little food or water.

"What will you do with food or water?" she was asked.

That voice was always there, teasing, tormenting, in the faint sound of that door being opened, then closed once more, the lock set, and the surrounding darkness for companions.

There were other sounds beyond, faint sounds almost like the sound of weeping when the door lingered open for a few seconds, then silenced once more. And then she alone again.

"What are you doing?"

The words stung like a blow.

"I told you not to move!"

That figure loomed up out of the shadows cast by the lights and came at her.

"I told you!"

The rage flew at her, then a blow that snapped her head back, and that single light shivered as her eyes watered. Then another blow, and she tasted blood.

"Now you've ruined it!" The words stung.

A shadow separated from the other shadows and loomed out of the darkness, and a sound. She attempted to cover herself, as if she could hide from the words, and that horrible glaring stare.

"Get rid of her!" Words that stung more frightening than any blow.

"There are places, you know them ..."

One

SUSSEX SQUARE

IT WAS one of those magnificent spring days when London had not yet given way to the sweltering heat of July, and my great-aunt, Lady Antonia Montgomery, had planned a family luncheon.

The guest list included me, minus Brodie who was off on some matter about a stolen shipment that no one was supposed to know about. One of those clandestine affairs that it did seem he was being tasked with more and more frequently by Sir Avery Stanton at the Agency.

I suppose the translation might be—the things no one else knew about, except Sir Stanton and the Queen.

Brodie and I disagreed on his work for Sir Stanton—very much so. I had my reasons, that had everything to do with Sir Stanton and a certain habit of being not completely forthcoming about certain risks during a previous inquiry, that could have gotten Brodie killed.

He saw it somewhat differently, one of the few points we disagreed upon. Merely 'the risks of the business,' as he called it. Our private inquiry business that allowed him to investigate a matter outside the usual constraints of law enforcement.

In other words, areas that were often dangerous and subject to 'plausible deniability on the part of the usual government agencies,' as Sir Stanton called it.

Plausible deniability. There had been more than one conversation regarding that.

"It means that the Agency can simply deny a situation if something goes wrong, and you are at the mercy of some criminal sort!" I had pointed out, somewhat forcefully.

"It means there are aspects that I can assist with that might otherwise add to a far more serious situation!" Brodie had replied, equally forceful. "And there are other reasons."

"What reasons?" I had demanded.

He refused to explain that part of it, only that it could very well involve someone of very high position in the government. Someone who was in a position that might involve foreign governments.

I call the inquiry business *ours,* as I had been known to contribute from time to time after that first case that involved my sister's disappearance. Afterward, there were things I was able to contribute from time to time to his cases.

Brodie had described my involvement as a most unusual curiosity for crime. I have to admit that I did find it most fascinating. A new adventure, as it were.

I had previously taken myself off on a series of adventures after completing my education in France. That had included travels to the Far East, Egypt, Budapest, Portugal, and Spain, and encounters with interesting people.

There was that Greek situation on the Isle of Crete, of course. The young guide had been most ... engaging. Admittedly, there was a great deal of ouzo involved.

If not for the unexpected encounter of someone else, I might have stayed on Crete. For a little while, at least, until my next adventure beckoned.

I had gone on to write about my adventures in my novels through the character of Miss Emma Fortescue. That had brought me into my working relationship with my publisher, James Warren, now my brother-in-law, to great success that allowed me to live independent of my great-aunt's generosities, or a man.

Then there was Brodie, in the middle of all my well-laid plans. There was absolutely no logical explanation for that particular aspect of my life.

He was not at all what anyone would have expected for a young woman of my 'station.' He was a former inspector with the Metropolitan Police of London who had managed to survive on the streets of Edinburgh as a young boy.

He was not formally educated. He was self-taught, as they say, with an education that did include some 'questionable talents,' as I called them—survival on the streets, certain insights into criminal sorts—and certain details of his early life that he refused to discuss. I could only assume a somewhat criminal past.

There was another aspect that my great-aunt had assured me was quite important—he could be trusted. I might have called it stubbornness. He was, after all, a Scot, and they were particularly known for that quality.

Yet, I had discovered that she spoke with some authority on the matter, even though the circumstances of precisely how she originally came to be acquainted with him were somewhat mysterious.

She had also insisted there was one more thing that was

vitally important, which I had discovered for myself—he made my toes curl, in the most unnerving, fascinating way.

I concede that it might have to do with the dark hair that was forever in need of a trim, that equally dark beard that made him look more than a little dangerous. But most definitely it had to do with the way he looked at me at the most unexpected moments. That dark gaze fastened on me, then the way it softened in that way that seemed to see inside me, past the walls I had built around myself brick by brick. And what was a woman to do?

So here we are, I thought, on a magnificent June day with my sister, her husband James Warren, and their two-month-old daughter Catherine, named for our mother.

The child had managed to postpone her arrival until after my sister and I returned from her art debut in Paris. Although I was not at all certain we would return in time, but dear sweet Catherine had accommodated us, I conceded, as I now wiped the remnants of drool from my shoulder.

Our somewhat unusual family of course included my ward, Lily, whom I had persuaded to come to London after the whorehouse in Edinburgh, where she was employed as a maid, had burned to the ground.

The bargain had included an education, a place to live, and prospects for her beyond those of a house of prostitution.

Orphaned at a young age, with no known family, she knew only too well what awaited an uneducated girl with no other means of supporting herself.

That was two years earlier. To say that the transformation was remarkable was an understatement. The young woman who now sat across from me sipping on a glass of lemonade was far different from that girl I had first met.

"Have you thought of having a child?" she asked. "You and Mr. Brodie?"

That question had been answered years earlier when I came down with a dreadful fever as a child.

The physician my great-aunt had called out informed her that it was doubtful I would be able to have children because of the lingering effects from the fever. So, here we were. And to be honest, I was quite content to let my sister continue the family line.

She was ecstatic with motherhood, although she had asked the same question a bit differently just that very afternoon.

"She is quite taken with you," she commented about her two-month-old daughter, as the infant's head bobbed at my shoulder, just prior to anointing me.

"Have you considered ... trying to have a child of your own?" Linnie asked.

I handed Catherine, who fixed me with a lopsided smile in parting, back to her.

"It would seem that Mr. Brodie might want that very much," she added.

We had spoken of it. Or rather I had informed him when he asked me to marry him, that I very likely would never have children after that childhood illness. He had simply looked at me with that dark gaze that softened.

"It's ye I want, lass. Troublesome as ye can be. Tho' I'm not a man of means. I pay monthly rent on the office, as ye well know, and inquiry cases do not bring regular money. Although I will admit that havin' ye about has increased the clients who call on us."

Such romantic words! About clients and rent payments.

It was the first part of it that stopped all my protestations when I could have pointed out all the ways that we were so very different. And what about my independence, my adventures, my novels? I argued with myself.

But it was those few words that stopped me—that he wanted me.

And who could argue with a man who knew my faults and habits and then had quietly announced that it was not enough.

He wanted me as I was, in spite of my stubbornness, taking myself off in situations that admittedly often turned quite dangerous.

Or perhaps it was when he told me that he had no right to ask me to marry him, that he had nothing to give me but himself.

I considered now how best to answer my sister's question about having a child as I wiped a portion of Catherine's last meal from the shoulder of my gown.

"I suppose a family would be difficult to manage with your inquiry cases," Linnie commented now. "Yet there are nannies available, and it is such an extraordinary adventure," she added as she handed me another cloth.

Not to mention the exorbitant laundry and cleaning bills, I thought, as I noticed the time on the mantel clock.

"I do need to get to the office." I made my excuses, fascinating as Catherine Antonia Warren was.

"Leaving so soon?" my great-aunt inquired as she returned to the solar.

"I'm to meet Brodie back at the office."

"Yes, of course, dear," she replied as she brushed the shoulder of my still-wet blouse.

"Have you spoken with Lily today?" she inquired.

"Yes, briefly."

"Hmmm." She hooked her arm through mine, and we

walked back into the main hall together. Which, of course, meant there was more conversation on that subject.

"She has spoken of returning to Edinburgh now that she has completed her studies here, rather than finishing in Paris, as you and Lenore did. She seems to think that she may be able to find someone in her family still there," she added.

"Although I have cautioned her there might be no one. I was hoping she might let the matter lie. Still, she is quite headstrong and independent," Aunt Antonia pointed out. Then a smile. "It does seem as if the boot is now on the other foot, my dear."

I caught the look she gave me. "I will speak with her. Perhaps I can convince her to wait until after she finishes in Paris," I replied.

"I suppose I might accompany her to Paris, if she could be persuaded. It has been some time since I spent any time there." Aunt Antonia commented, then with a smile. She looked at me.

"Or perhaps Mr. Munro might have some influence there," she added. "She does seem to respect him. I will speak with him about it."

I wished her well with that. Munro was a strong presence in my great-aunt's household and had considerable experience in his youth in Edinburgh. However, I was aware that he and Lily had been at cross-purposes more than once in the past.

He considered it part of his responsibilities toward my great-aunt to know where Lily was and whom she was with at all times.

For her part, Lily chafed under the restrictions, admittedly much as I had when very near her age.

It did seem as if the boot was now very much on the other foot.

. . .

I arrived at the office on the Strand and discovered, courtesy of Mr. Cavendish, that Brodie had not yet returned from his inquiries on behalf of the Agency.

I refused to call him by his street name, the Mudger, and over the course of my involvement in that first case had discovered that his name was Cavendish, which was far more dignified than the name he seemed to have acquired from certain activities while living on the street.

He had lived an early life at sea, that ended with an accident that had taken both his legs. Afterward he navigated streets, mostly in the East End that included the Strand, with amazing skill and terrifying agility, on a wood platform with wheels.

He had been with Brodie for some time before my arrival during that first inquiry case, a sort of gatekeeper and well of knowledge as far as what happened on the street.

While his early work for Brodie was somewhat of a mystery, his more recent work for both of us included valuable information acquired from the streets on more than one of our inquiry cases.

Brodie compensated him, as well as provided lodging in the alcove at the bottom of the stairs at #204 on the Strand.

That is, of course, when Mr. Cavendish wasn't keeping company with a particular woman who worked at the Public House across the way. And then there was the hound, Rupert as I had named him.

He was a scruffy bit of a wanderer that most usually smelled quite foul after scrounging the streets at night before returning to the alcove. He had acquired the position of *protector* for me, and had an amazing instinct for finding someone, most particularly myself, in the course of a previous investigation.

Both man and hound had become much valued companions and collaborators.

At present, Mr. Cavendish rolled toward me from the entrance of the tobacconist's shop, while Rupert was nowhere to be seen. After all, it was a magnificent afternoon, perfect for scrounging the streets.

"Good day to you, miss," Mr. Cavendish greeted me.

His choice of clothes had improved noticeably over the past several months, forsaking the tattered and stained shirt or jacket retrieved from a rag-pickers bin, for a clean shirt with vest over, and corduroy trousers rolled under what remained of his legs at the platform.

I suspected the improvement was no doubt due to the influence of Miss Effie Martingale at the Public House.

His shirtsleeves were rolled back with the warmth of the day, and a cap sat atop his head. Though his greeting was cordial enough, it did seem there might be something else there in the frown on his face. I glanced at the top of the stairs to the second-floor landing and the office where Brodie and I conducted our inquiry cases.

"He has not returned." It was obvious by the darkened windows.

"Not as yet, miss. You know as well as I do that work for the Agency often takes long hours."

I turned toward the stairs. "Is there mail delivery?" I inquired.

"Arrived earlier. I placed it there in the message box ..."

He did seem preoccupied with something.

"Is there anything else, Mr. Cavendish?"

"If you have a moment, miss ..."

"Of course."

I noticed his glance across the street and suspected the reason.

Over the past several months he had taken to spending more time at the Public House, which included any excuse to retrieve a meal for Brodie and me.

It was no secret that he had a particular affection for Miss Effie. Perhaps that was on his mind.

As Brodie told me afterward, when he first learned of it, he had considered talking Mr. Cavendish out of it. Yet he had not, as it turned out.

"How could I speak against it?" Brodie had told me with some amusement. "With the troublesome baggage I've attached meself to?"

I chose to ignore that somewhat pithy comment.

Now there was most definitely something Mr. Cavendish wished to discuss.

"I'm not a man of means, as ye well know, miss. And there are no doubt others what would be better."

"Better? How?" I inquired.

"Better for her, a man who could take care of her."

Ah, so we were indeed speaking of Miss Effie.

"I earn a fair piece from Mr. Brodie, and some other small jobs now and then," he pointed out but did not elaborate. "But she deserves better to my way of thinking," he continued.

"Miss Effie," I replied, to clarify who we were speaking of.

"She's a bit put-off with me."

"I see. And what might be the reason?" I inquired, since he very obviously wished to discuss it.

"I said just that, there was others she could do better by. I thought she might take a fryin' pan to me head. The woman has a temper."

"I see." I did see, perfectly as a matter of fact.

In that way I had learned about men, and quite often about Brodie, they considered logical reasons that in fact had absolutely nothing to do with a woman's considerations.

"Please continue," I told him.

He had removed his cap and twisted it around in his hands, no doubt uncomfortable discussing such things with, of all things, a woman.

"She doesn't see it the same way and called me a foolish bugger. I never heard such from a woman."

I did not comment on that, considering some of my choices of words.

"She spoke of things … Asked what I felt for her. I didn't know what to say. That's when she got her back up and went for that pan."

Not what might be called a romantic conversation.

"Perhaps she was hoping for something … more," I suggested, though hardly the one to make suggestions.

"What more, miss?"

Oh dear.

"Did you speak of your feelings for her?"

He nodded. "I told her that she was a good hard worker, the best the Public House ever had. Not like some of the girls in the pubs, there for other reasons as well."

Not exactly what a woman would like to hear, I thought.

"What about other feelings? That a man has for a special woman."

"She knows well enough. I go there regular and like speaking with her."

"There are times that a woman might want to hear more." By the expression on his face, I saw that he understood but was obviously not comfortable with the idea.

"You are a good man, Mr. Cavendish. If you care about her, you should be honest and tell her so. It is for her to decide what she wants, not you."

He winced, as if I had struck him. "I should tell her?"

I nodded. "Not that other part about other girls in pubs."

"A bit off-puttin', is it?"

"Somewhat."

"Aye, you're right. I don't suppose she liked that part."

He rubbed his chin. "There is another matter. I would have spoken to Mr. Brodie about it, but as he hasn't returned yet ..."

"Yes?"

"It's for a chap who has a shop over near Piccadilly. His daughter has gone missing now for several days, and he's worried about her."

A missing young woman? Far too common in this part of London, and as I knew only too well, not always with an outcome that one might hope for.

"How may I help?"

"Reggie Tavers is the man's name. He sells brushes to folks about the city and other business customers, the sort you might see with the street sweepers. He's not a wealthy man, but he has been able to provide for the girl after her mother passed. Gwen is her name, seventeen years."

There was a faint shrug of the shoulders.

"She's a bit headstrong, according to Reggie, fancies she'd like to leave London and travel. He knows about your work with Mr. Brodie," he added. "And he's hoping that ye might make some inquiries in Mr. Brodie's absence."

"How long has she been gone?"

"Over two weeks now," he replied. "Like I said, he's not a wealthy man, but he's willing to pay the fee to find her."

"Has he contacted the Metropolitan Police?"

That was usually the place to start, although I had found them to be less than effective in the past. In all fairness, it could be argued, and had been, that they had a good many crimes to pursue.

Yet the truth was they had given little attention to the disappearance of my sister in that first case, when I acquired Brodie's investigative services.

"A report was taken," Mr. Cavendish replied. "But there's been no word since."

As I had learned, in a place where crime flourished, particularly against women, it might be longer before inquiries were made, if they bothered to examine the situation at all. And as I knew all too well, the more time that passed after a disappearance, the less likely the missing person was to be found.

Mr. Cavendish waited, twisting his cap in his hands.

"I know what he can pay might not be enough, considerin' some of the cases you've taken for others, and with what the Agency pays Mr. Brodie. I'll add coin of me own if you would be willing to make inquiries about the girl."

"Of course," I replied. Then when he would have taken coins from his pocket, "We can discuss the fee later, Mr. Cavendish."

If there was to be a fee at all.

Two weeks since the girl had gone missing. That made it difficult to learn anything. Still, I thought of my sister and those agonizing days she was gone. I was willing to try.

Brodie appeared at the townhouse late that evening after I left a message for him with Mr. Cavendish.

We exchanged conversation as usual when he was off on some matter for the Agency, with the usual omission of any details about what he was working on other than he would tell me later.

"And yer visit with yer sister and Lady Montgomery?" he inquired over a dram of Old Lodge of which he was most fond, deftly moving the conversation away from what he was doing for the Agency. I went along with that.

"Linnie is getting on quite well with the whole thing and it appears that James is the doting father."

"And her ladyship?"

"If she has her way, she will adopt little Catherine and teach her all sorts of interesting things."

"The world would not be safe," he commented.

"She is quite a charming baby," I added in response to that.

"Ye no doubt made that observation due to your vast experience with the wee things."

I let that bit of sarcasm pass.

"And the most interesting thing, aside from the occasional drooling—it seems as if all that blonde hair that she was born with is turning the most interesting shade of red."

"A redhead?" Brodie exclaimed and sat back. He shook his head. "I'll have a conversation with her father about that," he added, "so that he knows precisely what he is in store for. Now, what of this conversation you had with the Mudger—Mr. Cavendish?" he then inquired.

"A missing girl?" he commented. "Among dozens, most which have taken themselves off with a man the family doesna approve of."

"That does not appear to the be case," I replied. "And it's been more than two weeks since her father contacted the MET," I added.

"And Mr. Cavendish asked ye to make inquiries."

"He offered to help pay our usual fee. And it isn't as if I have anything else to keep me occupied," I added pointedly.

That dark gaze narrowed. "I know wot yer doin', and ye know that I canna discuss my work for the Agency with ye. And dinna look at me that way."

"What way would that be?" I replied with feigned innocence.

"Ye know my meanin', Mikaela Forsythe."

He quickly downed the dram of whisky, always an indication of something more to be said. I was not disappointed.

"I s'pose ye agreed."

"It couldn't hurt to make the usual inquiries for Mr. Cavendish's friend. You know as well as I that it could be weeks before the Metropolitan provides any information, if at all."

"Then ye've decided to take the case."

"I've agreed to meet with Mr. Cavendish's friend and ask a few questions," I replied, then poured him another dram, to soothe the savage beast, as it were.

That saying usually referred to music as a means of soothing the savage beast. However, I have discovered that a dram of Old Lodge could be quite effective as well.

Two

BRODIE LEFT EARLY the following morning, with a final word that if he was needed, I had only to leave a message for him with Alex Sinclair at the Agency office at the Tower. Or leave a note at the office on the Strand. Not that he agreed to assist with my inquiries on behalf of Mr. Tavers.

I smiled to myself as I assured him that I would leave a message if necessary. I then dressed and called for a cab. When the driver arrived, I directed him to Mr. Tavers's shop in Piccadilly where Mr. Cavendish had agreed to meet me.

I did wonder how he managed the distance from the Strand. I imagined him putting a harness on the hound, much like a horse, then cracking a whip overhead as the London cab drivers do. Yet here he was, and the hound was nowhere to be seen.

"I spoke with Reg first thing," Mr. Cavendish explained when I arrived. "There's been no word."

The shop was open early for business to accommodate merchants, stable keepers, and street sweepers who had need of the variety of brushes sold there. The proprietor looked up as

Mr. Cavendish and I entered, a bell over the door announcing our arrival.

Reggie Tavers was short, with dark brown hair streaked with grey, a frown on his face as he acknowledged our arrival with a nod. In sharp contrast, his customer was a large man with thick arms, a stableman, from their exchange of conversation, who had just made a purchase.

I had learned from Brodie that there was often much to be determined by observing one's surroundings—where someone worked, where they lived, along with their manner toward other people, or a conversation that might be overheard.

I listened to their exchange as I slowly scanned the shop with its display of brushes and brooms.

The shop was neat in appearance for one that provided a workman's tools, that included an assortment of bins that held small brushes, with brooms of various sizes displayed on the walls.

It was a typical worker's shop, with a faint coating of dust on the stones underfoot, windows faintly smudged from a recent rain, and the rough wood counter where Mr. Tavers met with his customers.

Mr. Cavendish had spoken of the girl's desire to travel, and I tried to imagine what she might have seen for her future here— selling brushes and brooms. Perhaps caring for her father as he grew older, with a husband who might take his place when he passed on.

It would provide a modest living over the shop. But what of her dreams of travel?

Were they strong enough for her to simply walk away from the meagre living the shop provided? Had there been an argument perhaps, with her father who apparently had spoken against such foolishness?

There were too often difficulties in families, as I well knew. It was not limited to the working classes—a spirited daughter, a father with debts to pay, perhaps a loss of business coming out of the winter season, and the temptations for a young girl to escape. Perhaps physical abuse, although Mr. Tavers didn't seem the sort.

He was quiet and patient with the stableman who couldn't seem to decide which broom he wanted while Mr. Tavers made suggestions and explained the use of the wide birch-bristle broom compared to a wire bristle brush. The latter was a bit more expensive but would last far longer.

I continued to wait as the customer seemed to consider one, then the other, along with the cost. Then the man asked about Gwen Tavers.

"Off on an errand," Mr. Tavers replied, choosing not to mention anything more.

The stableman nodded. It seemed a casual enough question that anyone who had been in the shop before might ask. He then completed his purchase, choosing the less expensive broom.

"I'll be out of business before I need a new one with all the machines about," he commented. "There will be no need for horses."

Their business concluded, Mr. Tavers made note of the sale as his customer departed.

Mr. Cavendish had been waiting by the entrance to the shop. He rolled forward on his platform and introduced me to Mr. Tavers.

His customer gone, the shopkeeper nodded with a frown, his expression heavily lined.

"Cavendish here has told me about your inquiry work with

Mr. Brodie, and thank you kindly for being willing to meet with me. But you see ..." he hesitated.

"It's just that ... I was expectin'..." his voice trailed off.

I knew perfectly well what it was that he was expecting, and the presumption that a woman couldn't do something as well as a man.

"You were expecting to meet with Mr. Brodie."

"Well, with his experience with the MET and all ..." He glanced over at Mr. Cavendish.

"Now, Reg, don't go gettin' on yer ear," he told him. "Lady Forsythe has had a great deal of experience with inquiries. She was good enough to meet with you while Mr. Brodie's off on another case. You should be grateful that she is willing to speak with you about the matter."

"I didn't say I wasn't. It's just that she's a lady and not the usual sort to be poking around in such a thing."

I did suppose that was a compliment.

"In such situations, Mr. Tavers, there are often things that I would notice that could be important, things a woman would observe about a situation that a man might not. The fact is that I have contributed to our inquiries most efficiently. However, if my being a woman is a problem for you, then I understand."

I turned to leave.

"Not at all," he replied. "Yer right, of course. Beg yer pardon, Lady Forsythe." He glanced to the back of the shop behind the counter.

"I need to send the delivery boy on his way. A moment, if you please."

"That would be Gilly," Mr. Cavendish commented. "He's a good lad, a bit shy. Doesn't speak much. Reggie said he may be a bit off in the head, but he's a hard worker."

I caught a brief glimpse of Gilly as Mr. Tavers stepped into what was obviously a storeroom. He was of medium height, thin beneath a worn shirt, a tangle of longish brown hair tied back, with a long nose between dark eyes, and a curious expression as he glanced at me and Mr. Cavendish.

"It could be useful to speak with the young man," I commented.

"I thought you might want to," Mr. Cavendish replied.

Gilly nodded at something that was said, no doubt instructions for that delivery, and then set off out the back of the shop.

Mr. Tavers returned.

"It's usually quiet of a mornin' after I've sent orders out for the day. If you don't mind meeting back of the counter," he indicated the workshop. "It's more private."

"Not at all."

He provided a chair, and we sat at a worktable with Mr. Cavendish on his platform. The shopkeeper took out a pipe and lit it, the fragrant smoke mingling with the smell of wood and fuel oil, along with the overall mustiness of the shop.

Mr. Tavers spoke of his daughter—she was a good girl, had never done anything like this before. She was quick with numbers when working with the customers, and not one to carry on with men.

I then asked about her interest in travel.

Had she spoken of a particular trip she longed to make? Did she have a close friend she might have shared that with?

"She spoke of it. I reminded her that she was needed here, not taking herself off to some other country," he replied. "And how was she to pay for it?

"I'm able to provide a roof over our heads and food, but I'm not a rich man. And like me customer said, with all the new inventions and machines, I'll be out of business. I have to think of that.

"But I'm not unfeelin'. I understand this is not the place for a young girl with dreams and such. But I never thought the girl would just up and leave."

"You've made a report with the MET," I then commented.

He nodded. "A young constable by the name of Kemp. It's been near three weeks now, and not a word."

I sympathized from my own experiences with the MET. However, as Brodie had reminded me, it often had more to do with the number of cases rather than negligence over a particular case.

Still, my sister's disappearance two years before had been pushed aside as nothing more than a woman of means taking herself off in a fit of pique.

"Was there any argument or difficulty before she disappeared? A young man perhaps?"

"There was no argument, no more than usual about her wantin' to travel. And my girl is not that way about men."

As far as he was aware, I thought.

"I meant no offense, Mr. Tavers. Yet it's often some small thing that creates a difficulty when someone chooses to leave."

He shook his head. "There was no difficulty."

"Might I see her room?" I inquired after he had answered my questions.

He looked at me oddly. "What would be the reason for that?"

I explained that seeing a person's private room often provided some insight to one's thinking or possibly a clue that could be important.

He nodded. "At the top of the stairs. I'll show you the way.

The stairs is narrow. Take care, I wouldn't want you to take a misstep.

"Do you wish me to remain, miss?" Mr. Cavendish inquired, with a glance in the direction of Reggie Tavers.

"It's quite all right. I will continue from here," I assured him.

"I'll see you at the office then, miss. And back before end of day?" he added as a reminder, no doubt from Brodie.

"If Mr. Brodie should return before then, you can assure him that I will take care not to be out and about after dark."

He spun about on the platform. "I'll be on me way then."

I turned toward those stairs and followed Mr. Tavers to the second-floor room.

With the cases I had assisted in the past, I'd become familiar with all sorts of living accommodations—a flat in a rooming house, a room no bigger than a closet in some of the more disreputable places, or the back room of a shop.

There was always something that told one about the person who occupied such a place. I did wonder what Gwen Tavers's room might tell me.

As I began my inspection, Mr. Tavers made his excuse to return to the shop below.

"I'll leave you to your work, Lady Forsythe." He paused. "I ask your pardon for my comments before. It's just that no one has been willing to help, and you being a lady and all."

"It's quite all right," I assured him.

Gwen Tavers's room was simply furnished as I had expected, with a neatly made narrow bed, a simple wood chest of drawers with a few nicks and scuffs, and a piece of lace atop along with two jars. And oddly, a brush and comb, along with a round tin with a picture of a woman on the lid. Left behind, as if she intended to return?

I opened the tin and immediately smelled lavender.

It was powder with a small pad. It seemed that Gwen Tavers was a very discerning young woman, careful of her appearance, who had left behind comb and brush, and that tin of powder?

There was no closet, however a skirt in dark-blue cambric and a shirtwaist, along with a coat, hung at hooks along the wall beside the chest of drawers.

The one window was hung with lace curtains, and the bed was covered with a woolen blanket with a lace-edged coverlet. A narrow table and chair stood against the wall beside the bed.

A ceramic pitcher filled with lilacs stood atop the table, the blooms faded and badly wilted, and beside them a small, framed photograph.

It was a picture of two young women, expressions unusual. Most photographs were usually quite serious. However, both young women were smiling.

According to the description Mr. Cavendish had provided, Gwen was the one with darker hair in the photograph. And the other young woman? Who was she? And what did that room tell me about Gwen Tavers?

I sat in the straight-backed chair at that table and let my thoughts take in everything, as I slowly looked about the room with what Brodie called my 'woman's feelings' about such things.

I had once attempted to explain it to Brodie, that sense of something from a woman's perspective, a feeling when entering a room that my friend Templeton called the little tap on the shoulder from her muse, Sir William—the spirit of William Shakespeare. She claimed to have a spiritual connection with him. Not that I doubted her ...

I had not shared with Brodie that the voice often whispered at the most unexpected moments, preferring to simply call it 'instinct' about certain things I had observed.

"Ah," he said at the time, quite cynical. "Like the spirits the Scots believe in."

He did have a somewhat cynical opinion regarding Templeton and Sir William.

Yet, who was I to argue?

I had experienced many interesting and peculiar things in my travels, and my great-aunt often conducted seances at Sussex Square with her lady friends and claimed to have spoken with those from *'behind the veil.'*

What I instinctively felt now was that while Gwen Tavers was quite spirited, as her father had described her—from the orderliness of the room with everything in its place, including very personal things—I also sensed that she was neither foolish nor rash. I was certain she would not have taken herself off on an adventure without extra clothes or personal items, such as comb and brush.

That could only mean that she had intended to return.

I continued to look about the room for anything else that might tell me something about the girl. A book, perhaps a flyer from one of the travel companies that had first sparked her appetite for adventure.

Or perhaps, a wadded piece of paper, something tossed away in the small rubbish can beside the table? A note perhaps?

What might that tell me?

Possibly nothing more than a receipt for something purchased, or a shopping list. But the paper I found was neither. It was the front page torn from The Times newspaper three weeks earlier.

I had no way of knowing what that might mean, other than it was something that had caught the girl's interest. Still, I folded it and put it in my bag. I then crossed the room and retrieved that photograph. With a last glance about the room, I returned to the shop below.

Mr. Tavers had finished with another customer and looked up.

I showed him the photograph. "Might I borrow it? I assume the young woman on the left is your daughter."

He nodded. "That's me Gwen and a friend."

"What can you tell me about the other young woman?"

"Do you think she might know something about my Gwen?"

"It would help if I knew where to find her and perhaps ask her some questions."

"The other girl sells flowers over at the Garden. They struck up an acquaintance some time back. Gwen always went to her for fresh flowers. Her mother liked fresh flowers, said it made the shop look nice."

I thought of the lilacs.

"Do you know the girl's name?"

He shook his head. "Gwen might have mentioned it, but I paid no mind."

No name, but a photograph that might be helpful in finding the girl.

"Might I keep this for now?" I inquired. "I will return it."

He nodded. "If it will help find me girl."

I tucked the photograph in my bag. I didn't bother to mention the page torn from The Times newspaper. It might mean nothing.

If Gwen purchased flowers at Covent Garden, it was very possible they had been wrapped in that piece of newspaper, and she had then simply discarded it. Or did it mean something else?

"I won't take any more of your time," I told him.

"You'll tell me straight away if you learn somethin'?"

I explained that this sort of thing, finding someone who perhaps didn't want to be found, took time. Yet, I also assured him that I would let him know anything we learned.

He nodded again. "It's more than the police have done."

I had the name of the officer who had taken the report. I also knew of someone who might assist me with information about that report.

I found a cab after leaving his shop and asked the driver to take me to the Vine Street Police Station.

As expected, the constable who made the report was not present. However, I was able to speak with the desk sergeant.

"That is confidential information, miss," he informed me when I inquired about the report.

"You will need to submit a request to the main station at the New Scotland Yard. Once your request is approved by Mr. Abberline, you can see the report."

Abberline.

He had been the Chief Inspector of Police at the time of my sister's disappearance, an incompetent but ambitious man Brodie also had some experience with, that led to Brodie leaving the MET.

Mr. Abberline had been put on suspension after a previous inquiry case due to his incompetence and overreaching in matters, and had Brodie imprisoned. No doubt in part due to their difficult history. To say that I was not fond of the man was an understatement.

He was a loathsome, vile person, and I considered it an insult that he even breathed air. There was a time when I had seriously considered ridding mankind of his very existence. And now, he had returned. Past transgressions forgiven?

I knew perfectly well what the result would be of any request for information put before him. If I wanted to see that report, I would have to gain access to it by other means.

With traffic congestion as the afternoon approached, I walked several blocks before I was able to find a driver.

Although the hour was late in the day, I took a chance that someone at the Garden might be able to identify the young woman in that photograph with Gwen Tavers.

I was familiar with Covent Garden from visiting the market with my housekeeper to purchase flowers for one of my great-aunt's parties. She could be quite extravagant when it came to such things. Others might have called it *eccentric*.

Such as the Egyptian sailboat she had installed in the great hall, complete with water to create an illusion for a party she gave at the time. And then there was the Viking longboat she was determined to be sent off in, a fiery celebration when she passed on.

Eccentric was perhaps an understatement. Yet, who was I to argue with a woman descended from William the Conqueror, who had a number of lovers, no husband, counted members of the Royal family among personal acquaintances, along with a notorious highwayman and a smuggler or two, and had lived her life exactly as she pleased.

There would undoubtedly be a need for hundreds of flowers for sending her off in that long boat. But not for several more years, I hoped.

As expected, there were only a dozen or so vendors still at the Garden when I arrived, sweeping and cleaning up after the day's sales. Other stalls had been closed and covered for the night, those vendors gone at the end of the day that began well before first light.

I drew curious stares, a brief nod or two, and then an

inquiry from a rosy-cheeked woman who sat before her stall counting off bundles of roses.

"Wot can I do for you, miss? I've got several colors in roses, fresh from the man who grows them. If it's a special one yer after, it might take me a while to find with all these crates to sort."

In spite of the fact that many of her roses had not yet opened, the air was filled with the sweet fragrance of others. I pointed to a box of deep red ones.

"Ah, good choice, miss. Those is hearty and will be good for days if you get them into water straight away." She sorted through the paper-wrapped bundles and found what she was looking for.

"These is perfect, miss, and they match yer gown. How many can I wrap for you?"

I purchased a full dozen. "I would appreciate some information as well. I'm looking for a young woman who works here. A friend purchased flowers from her."

"There's a good many girls who work here. I know most of 'em."

I retrieved the photograph I'd taken from Gwen's room and showed it to her.

"It would be the young woman on the right in this photograph."

"That would be Lizzie. She usually works the street after collecting the flowers here. Most usually over at the Circus where the men purchase them for their wives, and others, if you get my meanin'."

Lizzie. In the very least, I now had a name.

"When will she return? I would like very much to speak with her."

She finished wrapping the roses for me. "That's hard to

tell. She ain't been round the past several days. One of the other women said she probably found herself a man to take her away from all this." She laughed as she made a sweeping gesture.

"Do you know where she lives?"

"She shares a room near here with one of the other girls. That would be Betty, but she's already gone for the day. She usually works the stall across the way." She made another gesture to the line of stalls opposite.

"She should be back in the mornin', although it's early before first light."

She had finished wrapping the roses and tied the bundle off.

"That'll be two shillings."

I paid, then thanked her.

Traversing London at end of day is always a challenge. I eventually found a cab just beyond the Garden and returned to the office on the Strand.

Mr. Cavendish was there, along with the hound.

"It's good yer back before himself," Mr. Cavendish commented. "You know how he is about your bein' out late in the day."

"It will be our secret then," I replied.

He waited as I paid the cabman.

"And your visit with Reggie?" he inquired.

"I was able to learn a few things."

"Then you'll be taking the case for the poor man?"

I nodded as I turned toward the stairs that led to the office.

"There are inquiries I can make."

I chose not to go into details of what I had discovered.

"I do need to speak with Mr. Brodie regarding the best

course to see the police report and find out what progress they have made."

If any, I thought, but didn't say it.

Up at the office, I laid my bag on my desk, then went to the chalkboard which I had cleaned of notes after the conclusion of our last inquiry case.

Brodie was not in the habit of making notes, offering the excuse that he needed to keep the details in his head where he could summon them at any given moment.

Most annoying.

However, that meant that I had the entire board to myself and my inquiries regarding Gwen Tavers.

I made notes from what I had learned, my observations, and possible clues—the wilted flowers, that photograph, along with the discovery of that discarded page from The Times.

I then sat at the desk and took out that front page from The Times that Gwen Tavers had torn from a three-week-old issue of the newspaper.

What might it tell me?

I was familiar with The Times, and a particular journalist with a somewhat notorious reputation who wrote for them— Theodolphus Burke.

It could be said that Mr. Burke and I had a somewhat contentious relationship. He considered my efforts at writing my Emma Fortescue novels to be an insult to journalism, while articles he wrote for the newspaper—he had been known to point out when he wasn't reduced to covering funerals—were of the quality of Henry Mayhew and Thomas O'Connor.

I was of the opinion that he was reaching a bit there in

both cases. That might have had something to do with our previous encounters.

For myself, I thought the man arrogant, bombastic, over-reaching, with little regard for the consequences of his writing, and merely adequate in his journalistic skills.

Writing funeral notices—names, dates, places—I thought were a perfect assignment for him.

As a chill set in, I lit a fire in the coal stove, took off my walking boots and propped my feet up at the corner of my desk.

Mr. Cavendish had brought round two cartons of food from the Public House.

I retrieved a bottle of Old Lodge whisky from the cabinet that sat beside Brodie's desk and poured a dram.

As the hour grew later, I put that second supper on a plate, then set it on the iron mantelpiece at the stove and poured a glass for Brodie, and a second dram for myself.

It was very near ten o'clock in the evening when I heard the sound of familiar footsteps on the landing.

Over the past two years, I've learned to read Brodie's expressions, followed by the usual questions starting with, *'How was your day, dear?'*

His expression tonight required whisky first. He reached for the tumbler on the table and tossed back a dram of Old Lodge whisky.

"And how was your day at the Agency, dear?" I inquired.

He held out his glass for another dram. It did seem very likely that his work to find the person or information he'd been tasked with had not gone well.

I poured as he sat wearily at the chair at his desk. Another dram was required before conversation. He sipped that one more slowly. His head went back, eyes closed as he let the whisky work its magic.

"You met with the man about the missing daughter?" he inquired.

"Yes, and I did discover some interesting clues."

I explained what I had learned, including the information about the police report, more as conversation than an attempt to draw any suggestions from him.

"It seems that Mr. Abberline has been reinstated. I expect little cooperation there," I added, with no effort to hide the sarcasm.

"Aye, best to make yer inquiries through Mr. Dooley. I'll put out the word to expect ye to call on him."

He had recovered somewhat from whatever he had been doing since morning, and loosened his tie.

"Be careful of Abberline, if he learns that ye are making inquiries about a Police case."

There was no need to warn me on that account.

Three

WE SPENT the night at the office and were both up quite early.

Brodie dressed in his street clothes, as I called them, with a felt cap and worn boots. In the past he had worn them when he was going into 'other' parts of London on some matter.

"You will be careful?" I repeated what he had said the night before. "I do not care for widow's weeds. And there are all the details to see to, not to mention what would I do with the office?"

"I would think you would carry on as ye always have, Mikaela Forsythe. No doubt with a half dozen men beggin' for your hand."

A half dozen?

"Not at all, Mr. Brodie. I would not choose to marry again, when I have already experienced …"

"Wot is that, Mrs. Brodie?"

If he was hoping for compliments, I was above that. Particularly when he refused to tell me what he was working on for the Agency.

"... Someone who shares my taste in whisky."

He gave me *that* look, that dark gaze, the expression on his face quite serious. He gently touched my cheek then kissed me.

I would have preferred more. However, he was already some other place in his thoughts.

"Be careful and take the hound with ye when ye go out and about."

"Careful as church mice," I replied.

"That is hardly reassurin', knowin' how mice end up."

And with that he was gone.

For myself, I intended to return to Covent Garden with the hope of speaking with Gwen Tavers's friend, Lizzie.

I dressed, finished another cup of coffee, then called down to the street and asked Mr. Cavendish to hail a cab.

A driver had pulled his rig to the curb as I locked the office and arrived at the sidewalk.

"Mr. Brodie said as how you were not to go alone," Mr. Cavendish informed me. "He was most insistent."

"Very well, then."

It wasn't the first time the hound had accompanied me.

Mr. Cavendish whistled and Rupert slowly emerged from the alcove that he usually occupied below the stairs. He stretched, shook himself, then approached with tail wagging.

He was such a scrounge of a beast that reminded me of hounds my father kept when I was a child.

"He was out late last night and asleep ever since." Mr. Cavendish winked at me.

"It's not the first time. There may be a '*lady*' involved."

I had never seen the hound quite so ...? 'Exhausted' was probably the best way to describe him.

The driver had provided transportation previously and

made no comment when Mr. Cavendish motioned for the hound to jump inside the cab. I climbed in and we set off for the Garden.

It was still quite early, and the traffic was thin on the streets this time of the morning. However, Covent Garden was bustling with sellers and customers when I arrived.

The stalls were filled with baskets of flowers and produce from growers in the countryside beyond London, as well as from the docks with cargos arrived from France and beyond. Shoppers, housekeepers, and others crowded the stalls to make early purchases before the day warmed.

I directed the driver to the part of the Garden where I had learned that Lizzie worked at a stall. I paid him, then Rupert and I walked the short distance from the main street to the entrance to the Garden.

There was more than one curious stare as we made our way through vendors and customers. The hound did make a curious sight, following along.

"Eh, miss," a bold fellow approached. "Wot might you be lookin' for? Flowers? Or somethin' else?"

Cheeky fellow. Yet, before I could respond Rupert planted himself between the man and myself, a lip curling back over his teeth as he growled.

"Wot is this?" the man demanded and laughed. "Should I be afraid?"

"That is entirely up to you," I replied. "However, you should know that he hasn't eaten yet this morning."

I turned and continued toward the area where Lizzie worked, leaving him and Rupert to sort the matter out. In very short order, the hound reappeared at my side.

"Settled that matter, did you?" I commented.

He looked at with me with that expression that could only be described as a grin.

"I thought so. Now, behave yourself."

Rupert was keenly intelligent, quite congenial most of the time, and we had been working on certain commands that I hoped he might learn.

Among them *sit, stay,* and *seek,* which the keeper of the hounds when I was a child had taught our hounds.

He obeyed the command *'down,'* I suspected because he had an aversion to most people with the exception of Mr. Cavendish, myself, and Brodie as long as he had food in his hand.

We were still working on *sit* and *stay.* He obeyed those two when it suited him.

As for *seek,* that was Mr. Cavendish's idea when I had managed to take myself off into a somewhat dangerous situation and Brodie had no idea where I had gone. True to his breed, Rupert had tracked and found me. He responded quite well to that command.

Of course, it might have had something to do with the food I provided, including the biscuits he was most fond of. My own thoughts were, as I well now knew about the male of the species, that he was quite amenable as long as his stomach was full.

But I digress.

I found the stall where I had spoken with the woman the day before. She was there, arranging a colorful array of carnations that had obviously just been delivered. The spicy fragrance filled the air as she unwrapped bundle after bundle and arranged them in baskets.

At a glance, I noticed an older woman at the stall across the way where she had told me Lizzie usually worked. It appeared that, once again, the girl had not yet arrived for the day.

I greeted the woman I had previously spoken with.

"You asked about Lizzie," she recalled. "I ain't seen her today. That be Mary Perkins. You might ask her about the girl."

I thanked her and crossed to the other side of the market.

"Wot can I do you for?" Mary greeted me. "I just got these lilies in this mornin', and only four shillings for a dozen."

I explained that I was hoping to find information about Lizzie.

"That girl!" she snorted. "Got her head in the clouds. Always goin' on about the travels she's goin' to take." She shook her head. "As if she can do that with what she earns from me. And then doesn't show up for several days? I may have to hire someone else. It ain't as if there ain't others that need work."

There were several more comments added to the criticism of poor Lizzie. In addition, I learned that her last name was Smith.

"Perhaps she's taken ill," I suggested.

"Ain't no excuse when I'm countin' on her," she snapped. "I got all these orders to fill and no one to help."

"I was told that she has a room nearby. Do you know where she lives?"

She finished wrapping another bunch the roses. "Yer might check with Archie, that's me boy. He's been sweet on her for the longest time. He has a stall at the other end—carrots and potatoes."

A most enterprising family, I thought.

"Is that animal with you?" she asked, glaring at Rupert. "They make a mess of things. Scavengers, they are. I ain't got no food here."

I thanked her for the information, then set off to find Archie, with the 'animal' trotting alongside as if he was going to one of the dog shows that were now quite popular. Although I had to admit, he was not the sort one usually found at such events.

The Garden was an amazing place. I had passed by it often but usually left the shopping to my housekeeper, Mrs. Ryan.

There were stalls with a wide variety of flowers from the countryside and foreign places such as France, and bulb varieties from the Netherlands, along with vendors who sold oranges, bananas, and pineapple. And then there were the street-side vendors who provided pastries and sandwiches for customers who arrived later in the day.

Overall, fragrances of the flowers mingled with other aromas amid conversations over prices as orders were taken, and there was the usual street conversation among those who worked the stalls, much like a village market, with a mix of accents, arguing, and laughter.

I eventually found Archie's stall. He was presently in the process of unloading baskets of potatoes from a cart. He smiled in greeting when I explained that I had spoken with his mother about Lizzie. He stopped work to bend down and pet Rupert.

"Don't often see a dog in the market," he commented. "They cause too much of a ruckus. Is he yours, miss?"

"In a manner of speaking," I replied.

Archie stood and returned to unloading the cart.

"Lizzie's a right saucy one, that," he said with obvious affection. "But not showin' up again will set me mum off on her ear. That's a full week now."

I explained that I wanted to speak with her on behalf of a friend and showed him the photograph of the two young women.

"I seen her before," he said of Gwen. "She comes here to buy flowers, and they go on about places they both want to see. I tried to talk Lizzie out of that. Travel on wot she makes here?"

That smile again. He was obviously quite taken with her.

"Aye, she's a stubborn one, when she gets an idea in her head."

I asked about the last time he'd seen her.

"That would be the week before."

I repeated the possibility that she might be ill.

"Might be," he said, thoughtful. "But she's a right strong girl."

He had been thinking of checking up on her as well and provided me the address.

"It's a pitiful place, a basement under the tenement at that address, just the way over." He angled his head toward the street at the end and the buildings that lined it.

"But she and the other girl have fixed it up some, and there's a window out to the street."

I thanked him for the information.

"You tell her when you see her that I'll be round," he called after me.

Just the way over' might mean anything. Yet, following the direction he indicated, I easily found the address just off St. Martin's Lane.

It was one of the older tenements that had been kept up over the years, with street-side windows at the ground floor, including that basement window Archie had spoken of with stairs that led up to the street.

I knocked at the first-floor door just off the entrance and inquired about Lizzie and the young woman she shared that room with.

The older woman who answered was obviously the landlady with a sign beside the door that reminded rents were due on the first of each month. I explained that I was making inquiries on behalf of Lizzie's family.

"The girl has been here, regular, when she gets off work," she replied, but didn't recall seeing Lizzie for several days. She reminded me that the rent was in three days. It if wasn't paid in full she would clear out the room and put in new tenants.

"There's lots of people want a room. You might tell her family, so they can pay up. I don't give no tenants charity," she sniffed. "The owner of the place would cut what he pays me to mind the place.

It was a harsh reality in the tenements around the poorer parts of London. I inquired if I might see the room.

"You'll be sure to tell her family, if she's to keep the room?"

I assured her that I would.

"I don't see as how there's any harm in lettin' you see the place," she replied and went to get her keys for the room.

"Is that animal with you?" she inquired about Rupert when she returned, eyeing him. "I don't allow no animals. The rats is bad enough!"

I could have pointed out that it might be helpful with that problem if an 'animal' like Rupert was kept about the place. However, I did not intend that I would be overlong inspecting the room. And then there was the look at Rupert that I'd seen before.

It was not a good indication that he would be willing to put up with the woman or the rats. I told him to stay on the front landing. It was far safer for everyone.

The landlady made a sound that I took to mean approval, and I followed her down the hall to the back of the building and a set of stairs that obviously led to the cellar.

Once there, she continued across the basement to a door on the street side of the building.

"I never had no trouble from them," she explained about Lizzie and her flat-mate. "They've always paid rent on time before. But it's a worry if the one hasn't been around for several days with rent comin' due."

Another reminder, which I chose to ignore and made no comment, as I had no idea when Lizzie might return.

The term 'flat' was somewhat of an exaggeration for the small room that she opened for me.

It was neat and clean, but just large enough for two narrow beds, one against each wall with a small table between and hooks at the walls for clothes, and pale light that struggled through the smudged window that faced out to the sidewalk and street beyond.

There were a few personal items on a shelf beside each bed. It appeared that nothing was missing, as if Lizzie planned to return at the end of the day. Yet, where the wall opposite was bare, the wall beside one bed was covered with postcards.

"That girl," the landlady exclaimed. "Always showin' me the latest ones she bought from a street vendor. Said they were places she was goin' to visit."

There were at least two dozen postcards with pictures from France, Italy, and Portugal.

I thought of Archie at the Garden. If Lizzie was determined, it did seem that he might have to wait a few years for her to return from places I recognized and had been fortunate enough to see.

I retrieved the photograph of Lizzie and Gwen Tavers from my bag and showed it to the landlady.

"Do you recognize the other young woman in this photograph?" I asked.

She shook her head. "I never seen her before."

"What about the other young woman who rented this room?" I asked with the possibility that I might question her about Lizzie.

"That would be Carrie Anne."

"Do you know where she works?"

There was a sharp laugh. "She works most days at a tavern, and most nights out and about with a man, if you know what I mean. But not here. I don't allow none of that. A man gets to thinkin' he's been done wrong with a woman, and the next thing you know there's a brawl and the place is crawlin' with the bloody peelers."

Carrie Anne. I made a mental note of that, obviously an enterprising sort, her profession unfortunately all too common with young girls who were turned out on the streets to starve, or worse.

A service bell rang at the floor above.

"I need to tend to that." She eyed me sharply. "I don't s'pose you have a mind to pinch anything, by the looks of you. Latch the door when you leave."

My visit at least confirmed that Lizzie had not failed to appear for work at the Garden due to some illness. But where was she?

With a glance at the wall covered in post cards, it would be easy to assume that she had taken herself off on one of her travels. Except that, like Gwen Tavers, nothing was missing ... not clothes, nor personal items—meagre as they were—that sat on that side table.

I tried to imagine Lizzie in this cramped room, attaching another postcard that she'd purchased to the wall.

Had she and Gwen Tavers planned something together?

If so, they would surely have packed their clothes and personal things to take with them. Yet, both had not.

I thought of my own somewhat rebellious younger years—escaping lessons at the exclusive French school for girls, preferring adventures to the restrictions of the station I had been born to. Yet I had never simply left, leaving everything behind. I was beginning to get a very uneasy feeling about this.

The landlady said that Lizzie's roommate, Carrie Anne, worked at a tavern by day and walked there. That meant it had to be nearby.

It was now very near midday, a time when taverns were open for business. It was obvious that Carrie Anne had not returned to the room the night before—likely because of that other *'work'* the landlady mentioned—though it was possible that she would be at the tavern for her job during the day.

I closed the door and returned to the main floor of the building and discovered that Rupert was no longer there. Not a surprise.

I was about to set off to find a driver, when the hound came running across the thoroughfare with something in his mouth.

I did hope it wasn't something dead, although he did have a preference for those, and of course, attempting to pry something away from him was almost impossible. I did not look forward to riding in a cab with him and something dead.

To my relief it appeared that it was a rather large bone. I would take a bone over the body of some rotting carcass.

He dropped the bone at my feet, a treasure to be shared as a driver arrived.

I ignored the bone.

The driver knew the district well, and indicated there was one tavern nearby, withing walking distance. He looked askance at me when I asked him to take me there then climbed aboard the cab, with the hound and the bone.

A young lad had just set out a sandwich board announcing that the tavern was open for business as we arrived. I explained that I was looking for a young woman by the name of Carrie Anne.

"Carrie Anne? She's in the back, gettin' ready for her shift," the boy replied, taking in my appearance.

"Is that yer hound?" he then asked.

In a manner of speaking. I told Rupert to stay, thanked the young man, then entered the tavern.

I have become used to curious stares when entering such places that have often been part of our inquiry services. The barman nodded at me, with a curious expression and I explained once more that I was looking for Carrie Anne.

He made a gestured to the room behind the bar.

"She's just there," he hooked a thumb to indicate the back room, and called out to her.

"Someone here to see you, girl. A lady by the looks o' her."

Carrie Anne came from the back room, in the process of tying off her apron. She was small, with fine blonde hair pulled atop her head, blue eyes, and a ready smile. I thought of that 'other work' her landlady had spoken of, a reminder of the poverty in the East End.

She gave me a curious look. "Wot can I do ye for?"

I explained the reason I was there.

"Lizzie?" she replied with a frown. "I ain't seen her, must be three days now. Could be she took herself off on one of those travel adventures she's always goin' on about with them postcards she put on the wall. Daft to my way of thinkin'. How is she goin' to pay for that?"

"Was there anything different recently in her manner, or something that she mentioned that seemed unusual?"

"She saved every extra penny, put it in a jar, said she was goin' to Paris. Spoke of it just the other week." She frowned. "Come to think on it, that jar is still there," she added.

"And there was an advertisement on the personals page that a friend told her about, somethin' about bein' a travel maid. I thought about it meself." She looked around. "Leave this place and me other work? I could do that—be a maid."

A travel maid?

"Did she mention the newspaper?"

"It's the one the landlady picks up, free the day after it comes out. She likes to read the personal columns, all them daft people advertising for a mate ... The Times, that's the one."

An advertisement on the Personals page of the newspaper, answered by two young women.

"I got to get to work, or Harry will dock me pay. When you find her, remind her that the rent is due," she said in parting. "The place ain't fancy, but it's dry and rooms that cheap are hard to find."

I thanked her and assured her that I would.

Rupert was where I had left him. Of course, it did help that he had that bone to occupy himself.

I was eventually able to find another driver.

"He's a pet," I explained at the look the man gave me. "From my dear departed husband."

I suspected the 'husband' in question would take exception to that, as he was more or less not departed nor was the hound a pet.

Yet, in consideration of ladies of my great-aunt's acquaintance who went about London with their small, fluffy pets.

Except perhaps for the size of the hound, and there was that bone.

I thought about what I had learned. It was not all that unusual for someone of means to have a travel companion, I thought, as we returned to the Strand. A lady on one of my excursions travelled with her maid.

That was distinctly different than advertising for a companion.

Four

BRODIE HAD NOT RETURNED to the office. Not that I expected him to be there when he was off and about on behalf of the Agency.

As I had already learned about this new *'assignment,'* the hours were often long and went well into the night.

The hound was content to retreat to the alcove with the bone. Mr. Cavendish had taken himself off to the Public House, according to the brief note in the message box at the bottom of the stairs.

I had notes I wanted to make, and I needed to make a telephone call to Mr. Dooley at the New Scotland Yard.

I left a message for him to return my call, then set a pot of coffee on the stove and unwrapped a stale biscuit from the previous day.

I worked on my notes in the notebook I always carried, then added them to the chalkboard regarding what I had learned so far in the disappearance of Gwen Tavers, along with the new information I had about Lizzie Smith. Then I stood back from the board.

Both young women wanted to travel, though apparently had little means to do so. Lizzie saved every extra penny she could, according to the young girl she shared that room with. Both young women disappeared without a trace, and neither one had taken personal items with them.

That seemed to eliminate the possibility that either one had gone off on a travel adventure.

I retrieved that three-week-old newspaper that I had found in Gwen Tavers's room and returned to my desk.

The Personals column, or the 'Lonely Hearts' advertisements, as they were called, were located on the front page of the paper.

I had never given much attention to such advertising, yet I was aware that my ward, Lily, found them quite amusing as she practiced her reading when she first arrived in London.

"Can ye imagine," she had exclaimed at the time. "Men and women putting up ads for marriage? I dinna plan to ever marry, but if I was to consider it, I wouldna put notice in a newspaper. There's no way of knowin' what ye'll get!"

Amusing as her reaction was, I was inclined to agree.

Now, as I inspected the advertisements, I realized they were quite entertaining:

MATRIMONY—Widow 44, with financial resources, would like the hearthstone of her heart swept and the cobwebs brushed away. Prospect? Matrimony. Respond #42336

The hearthstone of her heart swept? I could only imagine what Brodie might say to that.

And then another:

WIFE WANTED. Tradesman, aged 38 years, with a long-

established Trade which is most respectable; temperate, sober, steady man who is in every way qualified to render the marriage union desirable. Any agreeable lady desirous of meeting will find this advertisement worthy of notice. Respond #37642.

There were other ads for both men and women, for '*companionship,*' with several mentions of afternoon walks in parks, shared interests, and other 'possibilities.'

I could only imagine what those 'other possibilities' might include.

Most interesting, I thought, and as with each advertisement, there was a box number to respond to.

I continued to read through them, searching for the one that Lizzie had learned about. I found it in the third column very near the top of the page:

Seeking female companion for same, for travel and adventure. Age 18-25. All expenses paid. No whores or prostitutes need reply. Respond #41984.

It was quite straight forward, with the promise of travel.

The party who had submitted it obviously wanted a young woman of a certain age and character—*no whores or prostitutes.* And offered all expenses paid for service as a '*companion for same.*'

It was innocent enough as far as it went, and certainly enticing for adventuresome young women eager to escape the dreariness of their lives.

This had to be the same advertisement Lizzie had spoken of.

Had she responded to it? And what of Gwen Tavers, eager

to escape a somewhat boring and limited future selling brushes in Piccadilly?

The two young women obviously knew one another, perhaps spoke of their mutual desire to escape London, and had perhaps even planned to do so? That advertisement would have been a strong enticement.

I returned to the board and added another note about that advertisement beside the list I had already started, and then drew lines that connected the two young women to that ad along with a question mark.

Had both young women responded to the advertisement? Possibly another question—who had placed it?

The telephone jangled sharply. I went to Brodie's desk and answered it.

Mr. Dooley had received my earlier message. He had waited until he went off-duty for the day, then called from a tavern very near the Strand.

"It's best we meet at the office," he added. "Mr. Brodie wouldn't want you out and about alone late in the day. And there are other reasons as well."

Other reasons? Such as Chief Inspector Abberline?

He arrived in good time.

"He's not about?" he asked with a glance about the office. He obviously meant Brodie.

"He's on business for the Agency," I replied and poured a cup of coffee for him. He gestured to the chalkboard.

"I see that you've been making notes. A new case?"

"I've been making inquiries for a friend whose daughter has gone missing."

He nodded. "Must be difficult considering the past case with your sister."

"I am pleased to help, if I can. It does seem to happen quite often." I paused.

"Gwen Tavers is the young woman's name. A report was made with the police."

He nodded. "And you would like for me to inquire what's been done."

"It's been more than three weeks, and her father has not been able to learn anything."

"It's not uncommon," Mr. Dooley pointed out with a frown. "Young girls take themselves off, usually over a young man. Not exactly given priority with the lads at the Yard."

"That is precisely the point," I explained. "Nothing was taken in either situation. Nothing is missing—clothes, personal things, a hairbrush, combs. Nothing was taken. That does seem quite odd and no word from either girl.

As I spoke, he continued to study the chalkboard and the notes I'd made there.

"The girls are acquainted, and both hoped to travel. It's very possible that both may have answered an advertisement in the Personals section of The Times." I showed him The Times newspaper.

"This was found in Gwen Tavers's room, and the second girl spoke of an advertisement her friend had been intrigued by that seems to be the same."

Mr. Dooley took a sip of coffee then set it back on the desk. He shook his head.

"He said that you were like a dog with a bone—Mr. Brodie, that is."

"It could be helpful to read the report that was taken and find out just what has been learned," I pointed out.

He nodded. "Sad to say, this sort of thing—isn't a priority

as you well know, and often better handled by such as yourself and Mr. Brodie." He stood then to leave.

"I'll look through the reports first thing in the morning. It helps to have the name." He glanced about the office. "What about yerself with Mr. Brodie not around? It's well into the evenin'. I can see you home."

I assured him that I was quite safe. After all, Rupert and his bone guarded the alcove that led to the stairs.

I had decided to remain at the office for the night. It was certainly not the first time I had when making inquiries.

The adjoining room was convenient, much like a small flat attached to the office, and quite comfortable with a bed, night table, and chest of drawers that held extra clothes for Brodie and myself when needed.

I worked on my notes until quite late, typing them on the portable typewriter he had purchased for me as a gift with the usual comment that was hardly romantic.

"Ye are an unusual woman, Mikaela Forsythe. Most women prefer jewelry or a new gown to mark the occasion of a birthday, but ye prefer a typing machine."

And my response to that had been, "You were well aware of that when you asked me to marry you."

"A moment of muddle-headedness to be certain," he had replied.

There was more of course, there usually was. Something about he didn't know what he was going to do with a woman who wouldn't do as he asked, one who took chances, and would most certainly be the death of him.

He had survived quite well so far, I thought.

It was very near midnight when I pulled the page from the typing machine with my report regarding the inquiries I'd made.

Brodie had still not returned.

I laid the report on his desk, then put more coal on the stove and checked the lock on the office door.

Electric had recently been installed in the adjacent room. I turned on the bedside lamp, then crossed the room and pulled down the window shade.

I undressed, turned off the light, then crawled under the bedcovers, a faint scent of cinnamon there as I closed my eyes.

Nor had Brodie returned during the night.

Not that it was unexpected, particularly when he was making inquiries on a matter for the Agency.

Still ... I missed him, in ways I had never experienced before —his disheveled appearance first thing of a morning, the way he pulled me against him, the soft feel of his beard against my cheek, and other things that I had grown most fond of.

I was not at all certain when it happened, only that it had been somewhere over the past two years. And I had always been adamant that I would most likely never experience those things, least of all marriage. I did not need someone cluttering up my life.

All well and good, I thought this morning as I splashed water on my face, tied my hair back, and dressed. And a bloody Scot, no less! It was well known that most had a particularly stubborn nature.

'The best laid schemes of mice and men, often go awry,' according to Robert Burns.

My schemes had most certainly gone awry, yet in a most interesting way! Brodie was to blame for that, of course.

I had decided the night before that while I waited to hear from Mr. Dooley about the report that was taken regarding

Gwen Tavers's disappearance, I needed to pay a visit to the newspaper regarding the Personals advertisement. There might be something to be learned there.

How did it work? Did those responding simply direct their replies to a box number? How were the responses collected and passed to the person who placed the advertisements?

There was one person who might provide information, if I was able to encounter him before he was off and about for his next story.

Theodolphus Burke.

Just the name was enough to put one off, though I was convinced it was not his real name, but something he had invented to appear intelligent and draw attention. Much like the stage names actors and actresses adopted.

It was something I learned from my good friend Templeton, who was a very successful actress and went by that single name known by everyone who attended theater.

'Theodolphus.' It was quite pretentious, and the temptation was there to simply call him Teddy. Particularly after his dreadful behavior in one of our previous cases.

He was quite short in height—that perhaps explained the pretentious name. He was also quite stout, with side-whiskers, sharp, beady eyes, and a perpetually rumpled appearance as if he had just crawled out of bed, or possibly some hole in the ground, much like a weasel.

"Nasty little man," Lily had commented after a brief encounter.

And there was that other, somewhat disgusting aspect. He did seem to think of himself as a lady's man and had been most flirtatious when he wasn't being thoroughly offensive.

"The man doesna know wot ye are capable of," Brodie had commented at the time.

Needless to say, Mr. Burke and I had a somewhat contentious acquaintance.

However, I was not above providing a favor for someone who had assisted with information in our inquiry cases in the past, nor expecting one in return.

It was much like Brodie's working relationship with certain persons—Mr. Brown came to mind, a street person of notorious reputation with a criminal network across London.

Such was my acquaintance with Mr. Burke. I might be able to provide him a piece of news from one of our inquiry cases before other newspapers learned of it, and he assisted me with certain information. Usually.

I was hopeful that he would provide information about the Personals section of the newspaper—particularly, how many others had responded to the ad. And since it was currently the only lead into Gwen Tavers disappearance, I needed to know who had placed the advertisement.

I pinned my hair up, then gathered my travel bag, notebook, and that page from the newspaper three weeks earlier and set off.

It was well into the morning and quite safe that time of day, hardly necessary to be concerned about being out and about alone. Still, I decided to take a little 'persuasion' with me as I greeted Mr. Cavendish and asked him to wave down a driver.

When the cabman arrived, I provided the address for The Times, then called for Rupert to enter the cab.

"The newspaper, is it," Mr. Cavendish commented. "The lad doesn't much care for the place or that man, Burke," he added, referring to the hound.

"Precisely," I replied, and we set off.

If necessary, the hound could be most persuasive.

Five

&

THE TIMES NEWSPAPER, that popular enterprise of news and sensationalism, was located on Fleet Street. Newspaper Row it was called.

It was not that far from the Strand; however, reaching it required navigating the spider's web of streets that all seemed to run together between the City of London and Westminster.

I had been there several times in the past on an inquiry, including The Times archive in a nearby warehouse.

It was still early in the morning, and I had the advantage of knowing Burke's habit of arriving early to check in with the news desk, then determine which story he wanted to follow.

After our previous inquiry case, he had been assigned to writing up death and funeral notices, a bit of a demotion after a dust-up over a story he submitted that had mentioned certain indiscreet activities of a particular member of the royal family.

He did manage to salvage his position at The Times, but had been forced to write a letter of apology with the promise such a situation would not happen again. Until the next time, if I knew Theodolphus Burke.

The man simply could not help himself, which was the reason I chose to keep details of our inquiry cases in strictest confidence when using him as a source, except for details necessary to obtain the information we needed.

We arrived in good time, and I paid the fare. I was familiar with the cabman and there was no extra fee for Rupert.

"Makes no difference if it's one passenger or two," he had once told me. "Even if one has four legs."

Rupert leapt down and immediately surveyed the sidewalk for some prize that needed attention.

I stepped down with my travel bag in hand and paid the driver.

He tipped his cap.

"Good day to you, miss, and the 'fine gentleman' as well."

The 'fine gentleman' being the hound.

I entered The Times building on the main floor. Rupert accompanied me, having apparently determined that there was nothing of interest on the street.

I inquired of the desk clerk if Burke had arrived, and was informed that he had. I thanked him and went to the stairs that led to the second-floor area for the reporters who wrote for newspaper. Their desks lined up in rows, scattered with notepads, desk calendars, press schedules, several desks with telephones.

At one time Burke had a private office, but following his fall from grace, as it were, he was assigned to a desk in the reporters' pool. Burke was there.

While he had recently taken assignments that weren't about the dead or funerals, he had not yet earned his way back into that private office.

He had not changed in his manner of dress or personal habits. His patchwork growth of beard looked very much as if an invasion of moths had set to it, and his bushy hair was stuffed under a top hat.

As for garments, he wore what passed for a white shirt with sleeves rolled to the elbows and a garter above at each arm, a tie that was skewed to one side, and dark-blue worsted trousers that looked very much as if they had been pulled from a rag-pickers bin. Never let it be said that Theodolphus Burke dressed to impress anyone other than himself.

It did make me wonder if there was a Mrs. Burke. I thought the possibility highly unlikely.

Rupert whined. I was much of the same opinion.

"To what do I owe this very questionable pleasure?" Burke snapped as he looked up, having obviously heard the sound. "And there are to be no animals in the building!" he added with a glare.

"You may discuss that with him," I replied as I approached his desk.

Burke shook his head. "However did you get into the building with that beast."

"I walked in, and I would caution you that he is very sensitive at being called a beast."

"There should be a law against going about with dangerous animals."

I ignored that comment and took a chair opposite Burke's desk.

The 'dangerous animal' promptly lay at my feet and proceeded to go to sleep.

"I am making inquiries for a client. It's regarding personal ads placed in the newspaper."

Burke shook his head. "That is not my area of expertise, Lady Forsythe."

"Nevertheless," I replied.

He studied me with narrowed gaze.

"And if I refuse to assist you, I would no doubt find former Inspector Brodie on my doorstep."

"That could be a concern," I replied. "As I said, it is in the matter of an inquiry case. And ..." I let that dangle so that I had his full attention. "There is the matter of the Grantham case for which we provided you information afterward. It does appear that your position has somewhat improved since."

Brodie had persuaded me that Burke might be useful in the future when it came to information.

I was not in agreement. I would have much preferred that Mr. Brown or one of his associates simply take Theodolphus Burke down a long, dark street and never return.

Yet, at the end of that conversation I was forced to agree that the man could be useful.

"Grantham, a nasty business that particular case," Burke commented now. "And it gave me a two-part article for the newspaper. Now, what precisely is it that you want to know?"

"There are numbers with each personal ad that is placed. How does that work for someone wanting to contact the person who placed the advertisement?"

"It's a filing system, by number. The person placing the ad is given that number, and then places the advertisement with the number. Those responding to the ad use that same number.

"The responses are then placed into an envelope by one of the clerks in the advertising department, and the envelope is then picked up."

"How would I go about finding out who has a certain number? There must be a record of it."

He nodded. "That would be Mr. Charles, manager on the

third floor. He oversees all the advertising for The Times, including the personal ads.”

“And he would he have a record of the owner for a specific ad?”

“That is confidential.”

This from a man whom I sincerely doubted knew the definition of the word.

“However, *you* might be able to get that information,” I pointed out.

“You have a devious nature, Lady Forsythe.”

“No more so than someone who wants details about a murder for an article he wants to write before any of the reporters for other newspapers,” I suggested.

Rupert stirred. Burke immediately pushed back farther in his chair.

“The information about who placed the ad might very well solve the disappearance of two young women,” I pointed out. “And it would make for a most interesting story that all of London would want to read.”

Never let it be said that Burke couldn’t be bribed.

“The man who is manager of the advertising isn’t presently available.”

“Very well.” I stood. I was willing to give him time to find the information.

“You might be interested in something I came across regarding someone you might know, considering your acquaintances among the royals,” he said as I prepared to leave.

“It might even the score between us. It makes me uneasy to be in debt to you, Lady Forsythe.”

I preferred him to be in debt to me when it came to information.

“The inquiries that Mr. Brodie is making on behalf of the

Agency; it seems there is a person who might be of interest who lives in Hampstead, a wealthy person of some reputation who keeps a stable of fine horses. Most would never think of his involvement, but it seems that the man has some questionable acquaintances."

"How did you come by this information?"

"Lady Forsythe," he replied in that aggravating tone. "If I was to reveal my sources, they would no longer be my sources. I have to think of my career."

I did wonder what Brodie might know about the gentleman in Hampstead. Most interesting.

I thanked him.

"As always, a pleasure," he drily commented. "I will send word when I have information regarding the advertisement."

It seemed that was the best I could hope for.

"And you will be certain to take the animal with you."

I whistled for the hound. He stood, stared at Burke, for several moments before finally turning and following me.

At this early hour in the morning, it was quite easy to find a cab. I waved down a driver, and the hound and I returned to the office on the Strand.

Mr. Cavendish greeted us when we arrived.

"Mr. Dooley brought round an envelope for you," He indicated the message box at the stairs that led to the office. "Said you were to have it straight away when you returned, and then leave a message for him to pick it up after."

I retrieved a sealed envelope from the box, then looked to the top of the stairs.

"Has Mr. Brodie returned?"

"He's not, miss."

I took the stairs to the second floor and unlocked the office door. The day had slowly warmed, and I left the door open as I went to my desk. I opened the envelope.

Mr. Dooley had enclosed a note along with several folded papers.

I enclosed the report you requested, and another that might be of interest. I spoke with the constable who took the Tavers report. There has been no development in the case. I must have these back as soon as possible.

I was not surprised. The disappearance of a young woman of the lower class hardly caused a stir. I set aside his note and opened the first report. It was in the matter of a missing person by the name of Gwen Tavers.

I read through the information with the usual details—when Gwen was reported missing by her father, with no known incidents to cause the disappearance, along with a description of Gwen that included height, approximate weight, color of her hair and eyes, age, a scar on her left hand from a childhood accident, the names of her father and his delivery boy, along with the address of the shop.

They were details I was already aware of, and there had been no developments in the time since, according to the note Mr. Dooley had left. I reached for the other report that he had included.

It was also a report about the disappearance of a young woman two months earlier than Gwen Tavers's disappearance, a young woman by the name of Charlotte Davies.

She was 18 years of age, with blonde hair and green eyes, and about the same height and weight as Gwen Tavers.

According to the report taken by a constable at the time, it appeared she had disappeared under almost identical circumstances. When questioned about any known difficulties within the family, the young woman's father had replied, 'Only the usual among young people.'

Whatever that might mean.

There was an additional notation about a planned trip to Brighton with another young woman that had been cancelled. But no comment if that created a difficulty.

The other young woman, by the name of Emily Walker, a family acquaintance, had been questioned by the family but was unable to provide any additional information. She had not seen Charlotte for several days before her disappearance.

I glanced down at the name of the person who had made the report—Commissioner Harold E. Davies. A relation of Charlotte Davies?

I sat back in the chair at my desk and stared at the two reports.

Three young women, approximately the same age, had disappeared within the past three months. Nothing was taken with them, which indicated that they had merely stepped out one afternoon, intending to return.

What did that tell me? Something? Nothing?

I did wish that Brodie was here. I would have liked his thoughts regarding everything that I had learned.

However, since I was on my own in this, I needed to determine the next step.

With those reports in hand, I went to the chalkboard and made a new column of notes regarding Charlotte Davies's disappearance.

I noted the similarities between the three young women, who seemed to have a great deal in common in spite of their differences in class.

I then made side notes on the board with information that

might be useful, most particularly the name of Charlotte Davies's friend with whom she'd made plans to travel to Brighton.

It might be important to speak with both her father and mother. They were obviously a family of some means, considering that address at Covington Place in Marylebone.

There was one person I could reply upon to know something about the family—my great-aunt, who seemed to know everyone who was anyone in London society circles. And a few outside those circles.

She had spoken of the fact that, with her connections and those she knew, she could provide enormous assistance in our private inquiries.

While I was very aware that at her age it could be dangerous for her to participate directly, I was also aware that she would eventually hear of my new inquiry case from someone in that large circle of acquaintances, with the inevitable conversation to follow.

To quote one of our previous conversations regarding a particular case, she had informed me that I might have spoken with her earlier about the matter, as she already knew about the situation.

For his part, Brodie was quite circumspect about the prospect of my great-aunt participating in our inquiry cases from time to time.

"She will do as she pleases," he had pointed out. "You might consider speaking with her first."

He did seem to know her quite well, in addition to being quite fond of her. He thought her eccentricities were most amusing. Especially the Viking longboat she was determined to be sent off in when her time came.

Speaking with her did seem the most expedient way to

learn about Harold Davies and the Davies family, which might provide some insight into Charlotte Davies's disappearance.

I gathered my bag along with the envelope containing the two reports, then locked the office door on my way out. Before leaving, I handed the envelope to Mr. Cavendish and asked him to have the courier deliver it back to Mr. Dooley at New Scotland Yard.

Mr. Symons greeted me at the door when I arrived at Sussex Square.

"Her ladyship is presently standing on her head in the solarium," he informed me.

Not an unusual occurrence. She was convinced that standing on her head improved her circulation.

"I do believe they are just finishing," he added. "I will let her ladyship know," he replied.

They? I could only imagine who that might include. Lily perhaps?

Calling on my great-aunt unexpectedly was often an adventure in itself.

She had never married, and proceeded to live her life just as she chose. And had been on an adventure her entire life, along with that unexpected adventure when she took on my sister and me as children to raise.

Therefore it was always a very good idea to expect the unexpected at Sussex Square.

The Egyptian sailboat in the great hall afloat with its own river came to mind. Quite clever actually.

There was the car track on the green in front of the stables, and the older part of Sussex Square that had once been a medieval fortress. It mattered not to me at the time that it had been closed off for several decades.

The walls of the old fortress still encircled all of Sussex Square, with parapets, a tower with arrow slits, and a sallyport. Family legend had it that Sussex Square had been occupied for a time by King William I, William the Conqueror, an ancestor according to family records. The fortress had never been breached.

I had undertaken my first adventures there. And now, Lily had made her own explorations.

"There is a dungeon," she said, quite excited after one of her early explorations. "Did you know about it?"

I did indeed.

I WAS grateful my great-aunt had completed her morning exercises, including standing on her head.

While I had long ago encouraged her to remain active and exercises were an excellent way to accomplish that, attempting to carry on a conversation while she was on her head was a bit distracting.

Aunt Antonia and her guests, I was informed, were in the small parlor.

At tea perhaps, I assumed, although my great-aunt's definition of 'tea' most often included a bit of Old Lodge whisky.

It was distilled at her estate in the north of Scotland and had become quite a successful enterprise.

I had visions of my great-aunt's guests becoming quite foxed after a session of head standing. However, I was not prepared for the sight that greeted me.

The small parlor had been darkened with the floor-to-ceiling drapes closed over the windows. Only a single light glowed from a side table and illuminated a larger round table and the silhouettes of six people, all ladies it appeared, who were seated around it. Cards were spread before one of them.

It did seem that my great-aunt was indulging one of her favorite pastimes—card reading.

It was quite popular among her circle of friends; however, my good friend Templeton had dismissed it as, of all things— theatrics.

A figure rose from the table and I recognized my great-aunt, dressed in a flowing robe she had made after visiting India some years before.

"So good to see you, dear," she exclaimed as she reached me and then looped her arm through mine.

"I hope I'm not interrupting," I commented.

"Madame Orzcy is reading the cards for my lady friends. Agnes Vandemere is quite fascinated by it all. She's never had it done, and she's having some difficulty with her son. The man is over sixty years old, for heaven's sake. Who cares whom he keeps company with? Or she might learn about a tall, dark-haired man." She leaned in and winked at me.

"What brings you here the middle of the day, dear?" She looked past me. "Mr. Brodie is not with you?"

"No, he is off on another matter." I frowned. "He has been gone since yesterday, something that he cannot discuss." And then on a thought, "Is Munro about?"

He might be able to get word to Brodie. They always seemed to know precisely where to find the other. It was part of that shared history from their days as boys on the streets of Edinburgh.

"Not since yesterday. He is off on some matter regarding a shipment," she replied with a wave of her hand. "I do leave those matters to him."

A shipment. Not unusual in consideration of her various business interests.

She patted my arm. "No need to worry about Mr. Brodie," she assured me. "I know all too well that he is most capable in whatever he is about."

"One day you must tell me how you came to need the services of a private investigator," I replied. It was one of those great mysteries.

She smiled. "He was referred to me by someone—I cannot remember who it was. You must admit that it has turned out to be quite interesting, has it not? And now, tell me the reason you are here."

It was always best to explain as few details as possible when inquiring on some matter with my great-aunt. She had already inserted herself into more than one case.

It wasn't that I did not want her assistance. It was my concern that she might be injured or worse. And at her age ...

We walked together to the solarium. She ordered coffee for me and a dram for herself.

"Now, tell me. How may I assist?"

I explained the inquiry I was making on behalf of a *friend*,' then casually asked if she was acquainted with Harold E. Davies.

"That would be Harold Emerson Davies," she replied. "Undersecretary to Sir Donald MacPherson, Foreign Secretary for Great Britain. A most capable man, Mr. Davies, and quite a boon to be appointed to the position as he is not a peer. New blood is always a good thing.

"I've met both him and Elizabeth Davies," she continued. "He is a bit reserved, as I remember. She is quite charming, from a titled family, though her father fell into some financial ruin. I presume there is a connection to your latest inquiry."

Sly like a fox, I thought.

"The name was mentioned in passing and I thought that I recognized it," I replied, but did not mention that the name had been in that police report.

"And that naturally required a trip to Sussex Square. Not that I am not pleased to see you, dear."

She was quite clever when she wanted to know something.

"It was something that I came across for the person I'm making inquiries for."

"Of course, dear. Now, about Mr. Brodie. You must tell me everything you know about this secret work he's doing for the Agency.

"Sir Avery Stanton has been known to do whatever it takes to get the job done. I suppose that is the reason the Queen set him up for the task. However, Madame Orzcy might make inquiries on his behalf if you would like."

I would like very much to know what Brodie was involved with. Not that I was worried for him. I knew that he was very capable of taking care of himself. Still...?

I remained at Sussex Square. It gave me the opportunity to spend time with Lily and my great-aunt, as well as an invitation to remain for supper.

The ladies eventually emerged from the small parlor, always somewhat of a misnomer, I thought, since the room was quite large. Mr. Hastings brought the coach around to take them to their various residences. As they were leaving, my great-aunt drew Madame Orzcy aside.

"Another reading if you please. You might be able to tell my niece something of interest."

"Of course," Madame commented as she retrieved her cards and we returned to the parlor.

"Most fascinating," she commented as she selected the

usual number of cards from those spread before her on the table.

"I have never before seen such an interesting arrangement." She dealt another row of four cards and laid them beneath the original seven cards that she had drawn, then studied them.

"These two cards indicate a problem that needs to be resolved. This one beside them indicates there could be some challenge. Let us see what the cards tell us about it." She turned over another card.

"Ah, the chariot and the warrior, very powerful. The one this card represents is forceful, determined, a man who can be trusted. He is always there when he is needed." She turned over another card, and looked over at me.

"The High Priestess—you possess wisdom and strong intuition." She turned over another card and laid it beside the High Priestess. The Devil." She quickly gathered all of the cards and returned them to the deck.

"That is all I see," she announced.

I laid my hand over hers. "What about the last card? What does it mean?"

"I am tired. It is sometimes like that; a random card appears …"

I sensed by her reaction that it was not without meaning.

"What does it mean?" I insisted.

She looked from me to my great-aunt.

"The Devil can mean many things, dear," Aunt Antonia replied. "A sudden change, possible danger … not unusual for you."

"There is more," Madame explained. "The Devil can signify destructive behavior, being trapped, danger from a person you do not expect it from."

She took my hand. "You must guard against unseen dangers." Then she gathered her cards and rose from the table.

"Perhaps the tall man with the dark beard will provide a wagon or carriage, and I will leave."

"That would be Mr. Munro," Aunt Antonia replied.

She stood as well and requested one of the footmen to inform him. I could imagine his reaction to delivering Madame back to her residence somewhere across London.

"Most entertaining, wouldn't you say, dear?" my great-aunt commented when she returned. "Of course, it all depends on what one is prepared to believe."

Of course.

"Is the woman gone?" Lily asked, finally making an appearance.

"Yes, dear. And quite harmless," Aunt Antonia assured her.

"Have you checked the silver and other valuables?" Lily then asked.

"You are far too suspicious," my great-aunt chided her. "There was no opportunity."

"I've seen others like her, in Edinburgh. They make their own opportunities and quick about it. You'd never see them take anything but it would be gone just the same."

"I believe that I can spare a piece or two of silver," Aunt Antonia assured her. "However, I will have one of the girls make certain that all pieces are still present." She turned to me.

"And you must stay for supper," she suggested after Madame had departed.

During supper I did inquire about Esme DeLonge Blandford. Mr. Burke had mentioned Sir Lionel Blandford, who had once been with the Foreign Service Office.

"I heard that she had recently returned with her husband,"

Aunt Antonia continued. "They have been abroad for some time on the Continent."

Most interesting. That might mean anything. Still, it could be important to pass it along to Brodie. He had mentioned that his work was finding someone of position with the Foreign Service Office. Sir Blandford perhaps? And was Brodie aware?

When supper concluded, I made my excuse to leave.

"I know that you're quite involved with your new inquiry case," Aunt Antonia said as we parted.

"However, do remember the art exhibit that is opening tomorrow night at the Grosvenor. It seems that your sister met the artist when in Paris for her exhibition."

Admittedly, I had forgotten about it.

"What of Catherine?" I inquired about my sister's infant daughter.

"Mrs. Albrooke, the nanny they have taken on, will be in charge and Lenore will be able to escape for a few hours. I must say that she appears to have taken to motherhood like a goose to water. I would not be at all surprised if there is another Warren offspring on the way by year's end."

As I have often said, my sister and I are quite different in many ways. She is very artistic, with that recent showing in Paris from which we barely returned in time before she gave birth to Catherine.

And since that was not something I would experience, the future generations of Montgomery/Forsythe offspring would have to be left to my sister, who, as our great-aunt said, had *taken to motherhood like a goose to water.*

When he returned, I had Mr. Hastings deliver me back to the

office to make certain that the envelope had been delivered to Mr. Dooley.

It was well past ten in the evening when I arrived. Yet, as was his habit, Mr. Cavendish was there, along with the hound.

He rolled out from the alcove, the night mist from the river swirling around him.

"Good to see you, miss," he greeted me. "Mr. Dooley made his way round earlier. He received the envelope, so no worry there."

I caught his quick glance to the top of the stairs. A light shown in the window beside the entrance to the office.

"It's not as bad as it looks, miss. He's had worse to be certain."

I was already halfway up the stairs.

The office was dimly lit from the light that shone through the doorway to the bedroom.

I found Brodie standing before the wash stand in the adjacent room. The wash bowl before him was a dark shade of pink. He turned, cloth in hand.

'Not as bad as it looks' might be subject to interpretation.

The front of his cambric shirt was dark with blood, as was the cloth in his hand.

"Before ye go off and get beside yerself, it's not as bad as it looks," he informed me as he wiped more blood from the source of the wound on his head.

I took a deep breath, then set my bag at the side table. I seized the bowl.

"You will need fresh water."

He sat at the table in the office when I returned.

I wiped more blood from the wound on his head, then cleaned dried blood from his cheek and beard.

That dark gaze met mine. "It's only a little blood. Ye dinna need to go at it as if yer smacking at midges."

Smacking at midges—the thought was far too tempting.

"There's no damage other than yer doctorin'—I've a hard head," he added.

"I have noticed," I replied. "Did you consider that perhaps you should not have been wherever it was that this happened?"

There was a faint smile just at one corner of his mouth. "Aye, it occurred to me, afterward."

"You might want to have Mr. Brimley see to that," I suggested as calmly as possible under the circumstances. "You might need stitches." The cut was quite deep and still seeping blood.

He shook his head. "He'd put some of that powder on it to keep it from festerin'. I prefer yer way when ye aren't the cause of more damage."

As I say, it was too tempting. Yet, I suppose it was bad form to strike an injured man.

"What of the other person?" I inquired as I set the bowl of water aside and went into the bedroom for the medicinal powder left from a previous encounter.

There was no reply.

I returned with the powder and a roll of cloth that we kept after one of Mr. Brimley's visits.

There was that look. The powder without a bandage obviously would have to do. I felt him watching me as I applied it amid that thick, dark mane of hair.

"You've been busy with your inquiry case, accordin' to Mr. Cavendish," he commented, as I finished and put the lid back on the jar of powder.

"I've made some progress," I replied.

"And the missing young woman?"

It was obvious that Mr. Cavendish had shared a great deal.

"There are now two women missing under similar circumstances," I replied. "And perhaps a third. I'm following information to learn more." I didn't go into details.

"What of your investigations?" I asked as I put away the rolled cloth, as if we were discussing nothing more than the weather.

"Oh, yes," I added, before he could answer. "I remember now. You cannot discuss it, even though you've been injured and there might have been some difficulty where it could have been useful for *someone* to accompany you," I added pointedly.

I returned the bowl to the washstand and set it down somewhat more forcefully than necessary. It was fortunate the bowl didn't shatter. I seriously considered doing it again.

"You were at Sussex Square," he commented without mention of the bowl or my sarcasm as I returned.

"A most interesting evening," I replied, somewhat more congenial since it was obvious he was not going to share anything of his work for the Agency, and asking questions would gain me nothing.

"Aunt Antonia had her ladies there." I did not mention Madame Orzcy. "Lily is doing quite well, as is my sister with the new baby. She and I will be attending an art showing tomorrow night," I added conversationally, as if it had not been two days since I had last seen him.

"Aunt Antonia did mention that an acquaintance has returned after some absence, along with her husband who was once with the Foreign Service Office. Blandford is the name."

That got a reaction I would not have expected.

"Just returned? From where?"

"Munich, according to Aunt Antonia." I returned to the office. "It seems that Lady Blandford has relations there."

I caught that narrow-eyed look of interest. I had most definitely drawn his attention.

"Is that so?"

"Of course, it might mean nothing more than traveling about," I pointed out. "Still, it does seem odd to return to London when the heat of the summer is about to set in. I would think they would want to remain in a cooler clime, yet there must have been some reason for them to return now."

He rose from the chair and poured himself a dram of Old Lodge whisky that he quickly downed.

"I could perhaps learn more about it, if you think it's important," I suggested.

"No need," he replied, that dark gaze still narrowed as those thoughts churned.

"Of course not," I sweetly replied. "You may come and go as you please, no matter how dangerous it might be." Case in point, that nasty gash on his head.

"While I am expected to take trivial inquiries, then wait for you to come back bruised and bleeding."

"Mikaela ..." There was a warning tone in his voice. I ignored it.

"And unless you hadn't noticed, I am perfectly capable of participating in Sir Avery's schemes. In fact, I could provide valuable assistance."

"Ye dinna trust the man—ye made that clear."

"Neither do you," I pointed out.

"Not the reception a man might hope for when he hasn't seen ye in two days, arguin' about such things." He attempted to change the subject.

"Nor what I might have expected either, patching up your wounds, and I am not arguing the matter, merely pointing out that you could use my assistance, and with information that it is obvious you were not aware of." I was not yet finished. I knew that if I was to make my point with him, I did need to do so forcefully.

"Aunt Antonia found it quite odd. It seems there has been much activity at the Blandford townhouse, servants appear to be packing everything away just as they have arrived back in London."

I looked up and smiled.

"If you're going to go about getting yourself injured or killed, dear, you might in the very least let me know so that I can acquire additional supplies or make the necessary arrangements."

Not that he was fooled for a second, yet it was quite enjoyable to see his reaction as that dark gaze narrowed even further.

"Tell me what else ye've learned with yer own inquiries about the missing young woman."

Diversion. It was a familiar tactic.

"Another young woman has gone missing. I hope to speak with the family tomorrow. Two of the young women apparently answered an advertisement in the Personals column of The Times."

And because two could play this game ...

"You were saying about the matter you are following?" I added.

He wouldn't tell me more, of course. He had already made that perfectly clear. It was highly important, with utmost secrecy, a matter on behalf of the Crown, and all that.

"Ye are particularly striking, Mikaela Forsythe, when ye get yer red up. There's fire in yer cheeks, and yer eyes."

More diversion, distraction, and ...

"That will do you no good, Mr. Brodie. You smell like a

goat, and you are injured, quite bloody in fact—certainly an impediment to any robust activity."

He sat back in the chair at his desk and emptied his glass.

"Ye know I canna tell ye more." Then, "I see ye've made yer notes as usual. Wot more have ye learned?"

I smiled and poured him another dram. I explained about my meeting with Burke, then turned around at a faint rumbling sound and discovered that he had fallen asleep in the chair.

I was tempted to wake him. He would be far more comfortable in bed and he was injured, though it hardly seemed to bother him.

As I say, I was tempted, then decided against it—aggravating man. Let him stay the night in the chair.

Seven

"YOU COULD HAVE WAKENED ME," Brodie grumbled over his second cup of very strong coffee.

"I did not want to disturb you." He was not in the least interested in food.

"Ye have a wicked way about ye, Mikaela Forsythe."

I placed a carton on the desk in front of him, food that Mr. Cavendish had brought from the Public House. Point made.

I then went to the chalkboard and added notes to the list I had already made. I was hoping to meet today with the parents of Charlotte Davies, and then return to The Times.

As helpful as Theodolphus Burke was, it would be even more helpful to know who placed the advertisements in the newspaper that both Gwen Tavers and Lizzie had apparently responded to. As for this evening ...

"Yer workin' with the man now?" Brodie asked, apparently having read the notes I made.

"Not precisely working with him, but he may provide valuable information."

"Be careful with that one. As ye well know, the man is not

trustworthy. He'll do whatever it takes to further his own career ... and other things."

Other things?

"Whatever is your meaning?"

He was much the worse for wear from the previous night, with his hair scraped back from somewhat sharp features that might have had to do with some discomfort from the wound on his head, along with the beard that was sorely in need of a trim. That dark gaze narrowed on me with disapproval.

"Ye know well my meanin', Mikaela. Ye are a striking woman and Burke is no' dead. Given the opportunity, he would more than likely try to have his way with ye. And I would be forced to permanently remove him from this earth."

Have his way with me? I almost burst out laughing at the thought. However, it was obvious that Brodie was quite serious.

"In the first place, I might have a say in that sort of situation, which would definitely not be to his liking," I pointed out. "In the second place, I have proven myself quite capable of taking care of myself, as you well know.

"And third, he is not at all the sort of person I would allow myself to be with in a dark room, much less tolerate anything ... of an intimate nature."

"And precisely what sort of person would ye allow yerself to be with in a dark room?"

"I do believe you already know the answer to that, Mr. Brodie."

He was quiet, in that way I have learned to recognize when there are deep and serious thoughts going on behind that dark gaze.

"Ye should know, that I would kill anyone who tried to harm ye."

It might have been the residual of our conversation the night before, or perhaps that head wound. Or it might have been something far deeper that undoubtedly came from that early loss and the years between, when he had fought to survive on the streets.

"Yes, well, you might as well take Mr. Burke off your list. He's a toad. I could flatten him with a single move."

That brought a faint smile. "A toad?"

I had to admit that our conversation gave me a moment's pause. Actually, more than a moment.

I knew there was little that Brodie was afraid of. His background had provided an education in survival. Still, there was that moment when he said quite simply what he would do to Burke.

Not for the first time, I wondered what sort of man I had married. Someone I knew I could trust, to be certain. A man who was afraid of very near nothing, or at least nothing that I ever saw. As for that cold, perfectly calm statement ...

"I suppose that you are off again on behalf of the Agency?" I commented, as I prepared a message to be sent round to Harold Davies at the Commonwealth Office at Whitehall.

"Sir Blandford's whereabouts, perhaps?"

"Some matters I need to attend to."

Which told me nothing at all.

"Should I expect you for supper then, dear?" I replied with no small amount of sarcasm, even though I already knew the answer. He looked at me, no words necessary.

"And yerself?" he asked, redirecting the conversation in that maddening way.

"I will be off with Linnie to the Grosvenor Gallery this evening."

He nodded in that faintly distracted way, his thoughts already on the day ahead.

I poured another cup of coffee for the both of us. He quickly downed his, then went down the hallway to the 'accommodation' room that did now have both hot and cold water.

When he returned, any remaining dried blood had been washed away, his hair wet, his stained shirt thrown over one shoulder. Dressed simply in trousers, boots, and nothing more.

Speaking of distractions ...

He was quite a stirring sight, his body lean with a few marks from 'past encounters,' as he called them. And a reminder of that other reason I had agreed to marry him.

"Take the hound with ye," he reminded me.

"I cannot very well take him to the gallery," I pointed out. "I shall be quite safe. James is to collect us afterward and will see me back to Mayfair."

When he would have returned to the adjacent room, no doubt in search of a clean shirt, he stopped. The glare was gone, replaced by another expression—soft at the edges and thoughtful.

"He may be your publisher, but he doesna know you as I do." He touched my cheek. "And yer way of gettin' yerself into trouble."

I gave him an innocent look. "Whatever do you mean?"

"Aye, goin' off on yer own where ye shouldna."

"Only when you are not available, or otherwise occupied."

"Ye with yer proper words and yer stubbornness. Ye mean more to me than my life, Mikaela Forsythe."

"No one is asking that of you," I pointed out.

I never knew what to say in these moments when he said

something like that, hardly romantic. Yet the words meant far more.

"You might remain for a short while longer this morning," I suggested.

That smile.

"It would be longer than a short while, lass."

But not this morning.

"Then you must promise to come back in one piece, and that includes any further injury or loss of blood."

"Are ye concerned that I might not be able to perform my responsibilities?"

Responsibilities, was it?

He brushed my lips with his fingers, a gesture that always had a way of cooling any anger between us.

When he returned from the bedroom, he was fully clothed and went to the drawer in the cabinet where he usually kept his revolver and retrieved additional bullets.

I wanted to tell him once more to be careful, yet I knew what his response would be.

"Ye as well, lass," he said upon leaving, as if he had read my thoughts. "And I thank ye kindly for the information."

After Brodie departed, I had Mr. Cavendish take a message for the courier service to be delivered to Charlotte Davies's father at Whitehall.

In the event he failed to respond, I was prepared to call upon Mrs. Davies. It was important to determine if there was a similarity to the disappearances of Gwen Tavers and Lizzie Smith.

I wanted next to return to The Times office to learn who had placed that advertisement. It might very well provide a clue into the disappearances of the young women—not that I was looking forward to another meeting with Theodolphus Burke.

I dressed for the day, then closed and locked the office door. I gave the message for Mr. Davies to Mr. Cavendish.

"Will you be returning soon, miss?"

I explained that I was going to call on Mr. Burke again, and then would return to see if there was any response to the message I wanted to have the courier deliver.

I assured him that I was making progress on behalf of Gwen Tavers. Although as the days passed, I wished that I had more information.

"Burke," he snorted. "That one. Claims to be the eyes and ears of London. To my way of thinkin' he stirs up trouble to sell more papers. Nothin' more than a busybody old woman. No insult intended, miss."

"None taken, Mr. Cavendish."

It was hardly late in the morning when I arrived at the newspaper offices; still, I was informed that Mr. Burke was not presently there. I then inquired about Mr. Charles in the advertising department, and discovered that he was indeed in the building.

"If it's regarding advertising, I can have one of the clerks meet with you," the desk attendant informed me.

I merely nodded and proceeded to the lift. Upon arriving at the third floor, I encountered a woman at a desk who was obviously one of those clerks, as she rose from the typewriting machine on her desk. I replied to her that I was there to meet with Mr. Charles. She informed me that she could assist me with whatever I needed for advertising.

"Mr. Charles is responsible for all advertising for the newspaper, is he not?" I persisted.

"He is," the young woman replied. "However ..."

She was only doing as she was instructed. However, I have found that a somewhat creative response—Brodie would call it a lie—often goes a long way when it comes to acquiring information.

"I do have an appointment with him, if you will please inform him."

"An appointment? Yes, of course," she replied. "And your name, miss?"

"Lady Forsythe."

Even though I rarely referred to my title, it was usually sufficient to achieve the purpose.

"Lady Forsythe?" Mr. Charles greeted me with a somewhat perplexed expression. "You have an appointment?"

"Not precisely. But I do need your assistance. I was told you can provide the information that I am looking for. It is regarding an advertisement which has caused a certain difficulty in the family.

"It appears as if a certain young lady has responded to it, and I wish to contact the person who placed it, to explain that it was made in error," I added.

"I see. I do understand your concerns." He asked me to accompany him to a nearby office.

"You must understand that once the responses are received, they are turned over to the person who placed the advertisement. They own the information, as it were."

"That is precisely the reason that I need to meet with that person directly so that it will cause no further difficulty."

"It is highly irregular to provide that information. Many of our advertisers choose to remain anonymous for a variety of reasons."

"I must insist, sir." I was reluctant to make threats, still it was possibly an important clue.

"Unless it is necessary for me to have my legal representative make a formal request?" I added.

"Not at all," he assured me, apologetic. "If you will provide me the number regarding the advertisement I will see what information we have."

I provided the box number from the advertising page I had found in Gwen Tavers's room.

"It seems that the advertisement was made anonymously," he informed me when he returned. "That is not unusual, as privacy is important for many of those who place advertisements."

As with one seeking a secret liaison perhaps, or some other arrangement that might be illicit?

It apparently was quite common. And in this situation?

"Was there an address for the responses to be sent?" I then asked.

"No address is shown in the record. It would seem that the responses were retrieved quite promptly after the advertisements appeared."

"Did that person provide a name?"

Again he replied, "I'm sorry, no." He apologized. "It is not necessary to provide a name or address. A ticket with the box number is provided when the advertisement is placed. When one wishes to retrieve the responses, they provide that ticket or ticket number. Again, that is for ..."

"Yes, for privacy, I quite understand," I replied. "When did the advertisement appear last?"

"That would have been Thursday past."

I nodded. "And it will appear again when?"

"That would be the forthcoming Thursday, unless the customer cancels it."

"When are the responses usually collected?" I then asked.

He looked at his log book. "According to our records over the last several weeks, it has been the day after. Very prompt."

"And responses that arrive after that?"

"Those are held until the following week unless the customer calls again, which has not happened in this instance. It would be recorded here."

A customer with no name, only that box number, who retrieved responses to the advertisement that were received. And then?

"How might the customer contact those who reply to the advertisement?"

"For some, a place to meet is usually arranged between the customer and the person who responds to the advertisement."

I had hoped to learn more. Still, disappointing as the information was, at least I knew now how one went about placing ads and then making contact with those who make inquiries in turn.

I thanked him for his time.

It was very near midday when I returned to the Strand. I hadn't eaten since the previous evening and went first to the Public House. Miss Effie greeted me with a smile from across the crowded pub.

"Mr. Cavendish was here earlier," she informed me as she made her way across with a tray in hand and two lunch plates.

"Will you be wanting lunch cartons then?"

"Just one. Mr. Brodie is presently away on an inquiry."

She nodded. "Right away, miss."

She delivered lunch to two men, then paused before returning to the counter.

"There is a matter I would like to speak with you about, miss. If you have the time. It's about Mr. Cavendish."

I nodded, and she hurried off at a shout from Mr. Sturgess behind the counter that another order was ready.

It was several minutes before she returned, wiping her brow with the edge of her apron.

She was a pleasant-looking woman, with wisps of grey hair tucked behind her ears, her cheeks flushed from the warmth inside the pub and the orders that kept her moving quickly.

"It will be just a few minutes," she explained about my lunch order. She leaned closer. "There don't seem to be a proper time with me working here, and you and Mr. Brodie off on your inquiry cases."

A nearby shout for more ale brought a frown, and she was off once more, apron flapping about her, much like a bird about to take flight.

She was gone for several minutes, emerged once more with a carton, my take-away lunch in hand.

"Midday is our busiest time," she said by way of apology, as she handed me the carton. "There never seems to be a good time to ask." She seized the edges of her apron and fanned herself.

"I was married before, you know. Lost me husband to the fever some time ago. A good man ..."

I did know that she was a single woman, but not the details of it. She had been on her own since and was extremely hard-working.

"It's just that one never thinks about gettin' that lucky twice, you know?" At another shout for more ale, she tossed a comment over her shoulder.

"Hold onto yerself there, Mike. You haven't finished the last one yet!" She turned back to me.

"As ye might know, Mr. Cavendish and I have been keepin' company."

"Yes, I know."

"Well, it's just that I'm a respectable woman, and he doesn't think it's right for us to carry on in that way, if ye get my meanin'."

I had the distinct impression that I knew where the conversation was going.

"He proposed, you see," she continued. "Marriage? Can you imagine? At my age, and a fine man he is."

"I am very happy for you," I replied.

"I never had a church wedding, you see. Me and Eddie just went off to the local magistrate office and a clerk married us. I told Mr. Cavendish my feelin's about it, and he said as how we should have a church wedding." She turned and glared at the customer with the now-empty mug.

"I know it ain't proper, you being a lady and all, but I was wonderin' if you and Mr. Brodie would stand up for us in a church wedding."

Of all the things I might have expected, this was most surprising. I reached out and squeezed her hand.

"Of course," I replied. "And I would be pleased, if I can assist in any way."

She looked at me with more than a little surprise.

"I wasn't certain I should ask, you being a high-born lady and all. But Mr. Cavendish said that made no difference." She looked back at the customer who was apparently about to succumb from a badly parched throat.

"I need to get back to work. Thanks be to you again, miss."

A proper church wedding. I smiled as I returned to the office.

Mr. Cavendish was there. As I greeted him, I imagined him in a suit of clothes and Miss Effie in an appropriate gown.

"A messenger brought round a reply earlier," he informed me. "I put it in the letter box."

I retrieved the envelope and immediately opened it. Mr. Davies very politely but very clearly declined to meet with me regarding such a personal matter. The police were investigating his daughter's disappearance. He asked that I respect his family's privacy and their wishes.

Very well. I did understand that a man of his position might be in a difficult situation, but I found it impossible to comprehend that he wouldn't want to explore every possibility in finding his daughter.

"Is there a difficulty, miss?" Mr. Cavendish inquired.

"Not at all," I replied.

I would have mentioned my conversation with Miss Effie, but decided that it was perhaps best to let her speak with him about it.

"Will you be working late? Mr. Brodie mentioned it before he left this morning."

"I have some notes to make before I leave for Mayfair. I'll be attending a gathering with my sister this evening."

"Right ye are, miss. Let me know when yer ready to leave and I'll make certain to have a driver for you."

I turned toward the stairs. In spite of Mr. Davies's very brief, courteous reply, I was not about to be set aside in my efforts to learn if his daughter's disappearance might be connected to the disappearances of Gwen Tavers and Lizzie Smith.

There was always more than one way to find out.

Eight

I RETURNED to the townhouse late in the afternoon and informed Mrs. Ryan of my plans for the evening.

"I'll prepare an early supper then. And yer sister, Mrs. Warren?" she inquired.

"An evening out. I believe she may be trying to escape for a few hours."

That brought a smile. "I remember it well, from when my Mary was a baby." She paused at a memory that I knew was still painful and undoubtedly always would be.

"I have a gift for the wee thing. If you would be good enough to give it to Miss Lenore. It's a small thing, but I thought of her when I saw it."

She was quite fond of my sister. They had experienced that tragic loss together—the death of Mary Ryan, who had been my sister's personal maid, found murdered after both disappeared.

It was that first inquiry case when I refused to be set aside by the Metropolitan Police, one Chief Inspector Abberline, as an overwrought, meddlesome woman. It was also the first time I worked with Brodie, much to his disapproval at the time.

A great many things had certainly changed over the few years since with Brodie now a part of my life—most of the time. Not that I was complaining.

"And what of Mr. Brodie?" she inquired. "Will he be joining you this evening?"

"He is off on some business for a client," I replied, and said nothing more.

I worked at my writing desk in the front parlor, updating the notebook that I always carried.

I then went upstairs to select a gown for the exhibit at the gallery that evening, but not before bathing in the new shower compartment that I had installed several months earlier.

It was an amazing invention, with warm water pumped from a coal-fired tank in the kitchen into a copper holding tank mounted above the compartment. The only thing necessary for one to do was to open the valve on the holding tank and warm water showered down from above. Brodie was especially fond of the shower compartment.

But I digress.

I dressed for the evening and went downstairs to supper. Linnie arrived shortly after in somewhat of a dither, which I gathered had to do with leaving young Catherine for the first time and for several hours.

"I do hope James can manage. He was most insistent that I continue with plans for the evening. Can you imagine? A man wanting to care for an infant?"

I thought her quite fortunate in that regard. The male of our species was not well known for such domestic responsibilities.

She requested a towel to clean a spot on the shoulder of her gown where Catherine had anointed her before departing.

Bravo, Catherine, I thought, those were my sentiments exactly about art exhibits that were usually quite boring. Mrs. Ryan provided her expertise in taking care of such situations with a cotton cloth and a powder that she rubbed into the fabric.

"Baking soda," she informed us. "It will soak up a stain unless it has grease in it."

"Perhaps this was not the time for going out," Linnie continued to dither. "Catherine is still quite young. And if there should be a situation ... And now with this stain?"

"You haven't been out as yet," I told her. "It will do you good. And the stain has removed itself."

We set off.

"This is very exciting," she commented. "I met the artist when we were in Paris. He is very talented, and now his own exhibit with a collection of new pieces he's been working on the past year. And it seems that he will be in London for some time."

Exciting was not precisely the word I would have chosen. Yet I wanted to support my sister, and it was the first time she had been out and about socially since little Catherine made her debut.

The gas lights across the front of the building glowed and a sign on the street announced the collection of *Simon La Geness*. I remembered the name, although I had taken myself off during my sister's Paris exhibition and had not previously met the artist.

It did seem as if there would be an impressive attendance as the driver eased the coach into the queue of other coaches and carriages outside the main entrance. An attendant opened the door, and we joined other guests who entered the building.

I had attended the Grosvenor Gallery on other occasions, more recently in a previous inquiry.

That specific visit had begun simply enough in attendance with Linnie, Aunt Antonia, and Lily, with no warning how the events of the evening would endanger everyone. A particularly difficult case some months before.

"Is the stain on my shoulder gone?" Linnie asked as we approached the exhibit hall for oil and water-color portraits.

"Nearly," I replied. "However, I believe that it does add a touch of motherly flair."

She gave me a withering look. "Catherine has claimed my entire wardrobe since her arrival. It is quite an adventure, dear sister. You should consider it."

Yes, well, perhaps it was best that role was left to Linnie. I had visions of dark-eyed, dark haired, devilish little Scot babies and shook off the thought.

"You are a wonderful mother," I told her. "We shall leave it at that."

She smiled. "Catherine is so sweet-tempered. James has said he would like a half dozen."

A half dozen?

As we reached the entrance to the hall, Linnie showed a member of the gallery staff the engraved invitation she had received, and we proceeded inside.

Unlike that previous encounter, I was quite content to let my sister enjoy the evening, as we were greeted by people she knew in the art community, while I went my way and observed the various artists' works that were there as part of the display over the next month.

There were several paintings from artists I recognized, in both oils and water colors—all those hours spent in Paris museums and galleries while we were at school. And far more I did not recognize.

I was no expert; however I could identify the Impressionist style, and something Linnie called the New Impressionist Style.

We eventually found each other once more, as she informed me that Monsieur La Geness's pieces were across the way where several patrons had gathered and seemed to be speaking among themselves with considerable excitement.

Or perhaps *excitement* might have been an understatement, as I caught several comments of those who stood about the exhibit, including dismay, more than one exclamation of surprise, and a haughtily muttered, "What do you expect from a Frenchman?"

I was most curious.

"Oh ..." Linnie said, as we joined them and viewed the paintings in La Geness's new collection. It took her a moment to recover.

"The invitation called the exhibit "*Les femmes.*"

"I would say it is most *natural,*" I replied.

There were three portraits on display, arranged in a half circle to take advantage of the light, with the one in the middle raised on a platform.

"They're very much in the style of Manet," Linnie commented. "It has become quite prominent in the Paris art colonies," she explained amid the somewhat shocked comments from the other guests.

"They are quite ..." She seemed to search for the appropriate word.

I thought it was most entertaining.

"Provocative?" I provided.

"I suppose that would be *the* word."

Scandalous was another word that came to mind and apparently several other guests were of the same opinion, I thought with some amusement.

Some were curious, with questions for the artist, while some of the ladies glanced askance at the portraits, yet glance they did.

More than one sniffed with apparent indifference, yet continued to stare, much to my amusement. Others, however, were complimentary to the artist and showed a true appreciation for art, with questions about the inspiration for the paintings as well as his use of light and shadow on his subjects.

The particular technique La Geness had used was in muted tones for the background in each that emphasized the sensual lines of the subject in each painting, a woman very scantily clothed or not at all.

The painting in the middle of the exhibit portrayed the model with long dark hair, standing as though before a mirror with a small mirror in hand, her other hand raised as if touching her hair. She was young, quite pretty, with a pensive expression as if waiting for ...

What, I wondered?

The answer might have been in her costume or what there was of it. It was a long, draped gown in what appeared to be a sheer silk, quite revealing, with a bright red ribbon tied about her waist. Much like a package to be opened?

The tails of the ribbon fell to her knees and barely covered that most intimate part while the sheer silk emphasized her breasts, with nothing left to the imagination. The title of the painting was equally suggestive—*'Waiting.'*

One of the other paintings was a side-view of a naked

young woman, her face hidden behind her raised arm as she held up her long dark hair, her back arched, a breast exposed, the lines of her body sensual and revealing. The title of the painting—'Desire'—was as provocative as the portrait itself.

The third painting was also of a young woman, seated with a shawl wrapped around her lower body, her arm shielding her breast, her hair down about her shoulders and back. And like the other portraits, it was both innocent and seductive in what it suggested.

Yet, it wasn't the young woman's innocence, but an almost sad expression caught in profile, her half-naked body exposed for all to see.

"For heaven's sake, Mikaela. You're staring! It isn't as if you haven't seen similar subjects before in paintings we saw while in Paris."

Before I could respond we were greeted by a thick French accent.

"Madame Warren, I had hoped that you might accept my invitation. And you have brought a guest," Monsieur La Geness greeted us.

"*Oui*, my sister, Lady Forsythe." Linnie made the introduction.

He nodded and took my hand, his expression warm, perhaps even a bit flirtatious.

"I am honored that you would come to see my work."

I caught the overlong look he gave me as he held onto my hand.

"Most exquisite," he said then.

Not a word I had heard before.

"You must forgive me. The color of your hair," he said. "It is quite extraordinary. Other shades are often faded, or false. Yours is rare, the sort an artist should paint."

La Geness was of medium height, with a receding hairline and beard without the usual side-whiskers that were the fashion in London. His eyes were hazel green, brows arched in a tentative expression, one hand tucked into his pockets. The one that held onto mine longer than might have been proper shook slightly. He quickly released my hand.

"To paint such a portrait would be an honor."

"Is Madame here as well?" Linnie inquired, interceding as I had a particular comment I would have shared with him.

"Not this evening," he replied. He gestured to his paintings.

"Tell me, Lady Forsythe. What do you think of my young *ladies?*"

I caught the warning look from my sister, something she should practice for little Catherine. Most amusing.

However, I was not a cruel person and could soon escape to another part of the gallery for the next two hours.

"Each one seems to convey emotion—shyness, perhaps even a certain sadness. This one in particular," I indicated the third painting with the young woman wrapped in a shawl. "I have always wondered how artists persuade women to pose for them. Are they all from Paris?"

He smiled, somewhat indulgently I thought.

"It is not difficult to find subjects to pose. The difficulty lies in finding one that can provide the image that is in the artist's mind, an expression, or nuance. Innocence, perhaps as you see there, or a question that is in the look of the subject. It is often necessary to persuade the desired emotion from the subject," he added.

"And if you cannot persuade the desired emotion?" I inquired, curious at his description.

"There are always young women eager to pose for a few

coins. And if I cannot find that one young woman to be part of the collection, I am always making sketches of faces I see."

I wondered about the emotions I saw on the faces of the three young women in the portraits. Especially the young woman with the shawl—a face and an emotion from his imagination, no doubt from his studio in Paris. Still ...

"How long will you remain in London?" Linnie asked.

"I have found a residence here. It is old and has stood empty for some time, I am told. Yet it suits my purpose. It has a studio for my work that I hope to add to my collection before leaving for Paris, then New York in the fall." He turned to Linnie.

"And you must return to your work. As I am certain you are aware, it is an obsession that we have."

"I hope to take up the brush once more very soon. Although I must think of my family," Linnie replied.

"Ah yes, the child. I remember well from Paris." He turned to me. "And you, mademoiselle?"

Mademoiselle? The French were quite notorious for their less than subtle flirtations with women of all ages.

"I am not the artist in the family," I replied. "I do not have the talent for it." Nor the patience, I thought. "I leave that to my sister." I then made my departure to view the other paintings on display.

"If you will excuse me ..."

However, the truth was that while I had a passing appreciation for art, I either liked a piece of art, or not.

I did not proceed to analyze every nuance of it for some particular meaning, which was much like one's opinion, I thought. Very different from one person to the next.

I ventured across the gallery to observe the other works that were displayed, with styles that included the Renaissance, two pieces of Medieval art, as well as other pieces in the Impression-istic style, some which were quite bizarre by Cezanne, then quickly moved on, exchanging a nod or greeting with those whom I recognized.

I did hope that Linnie was enjoying her evening as I paused before a painting by Monet.

He was part of the Impressionist movement. He painted with loose brushes, and used light and atmosphere in a scene to show movement, according to my sister.

Of all the artists I was exposed to while in Paris, his paint-ings seemed to pull me in, as if I was standing on that cliff with the wind under *my* umbrella, like the young woman in this painting, *Cliff at Dieppe*.

If I had explained that to Linnie, she would have been astounded.

I smiled to myself. We shall keep our secret, Monsieur Monet, I thought. *N'est-ce pas?*

I remained several minutes longer with the 'lady on the cliff' with my questions that others perhaps had when viewing the painting.

What did she see beyond the cliff? Someone, perhaps? A lover? Or was she simply lost in thought, enjoying the day?

It was impossible to tell with Monet's style what he might have intended. To leave it to each person as they looked at his work.

I felt it at first, that very peculiar sense of something, that inner voice my friend Templeton called it—an awareness of something not quite discernible, but there nevertheless.

When I turned to continue on to the next painting, I noticed a woman some distance apart among the guests. She was staring at me.

She appeared to be alone, although I supposed that a

companion could be off inspecting another painting, as she continued to stare.

She had fine features, with dark hair coiled at the back of her head, and was dressed in a dark-blue gown. Her expression was most thoughtful, almost as if she knew me.

I slowly moved on then stopped before a painting by Pissarro, a French landscape that included a vineyard that reminded me of my great-aunt's property in the south of France.

I lingered for several moments, stealing another glance then turning back once more to the painting. As I continued on, I looked for her once more, but she was gone. I glanced among the guests but failed to find any trace of her.

I realized that I had been absent for some time, and rejoined my sister. James had arrived and she was most anxious about being absent overlong from young Catherine. I was more than ready to leave as well.

I looked once more for the woman I had seen, but failed to find her, as we made our way to the coach James had waiting.

I was too restless to sleep after returning to the townhouse. Instead, I sat at my writing desk and added notes regarding the evening in my notebook, including that somewhat odd encounter with the woman in the blue gown that was actually not an encounter at all.

As for La Geness's showing at the gallery that evening, it was difficult to explain my thoughts about the painting of the young woman in a shawl.

What was it? Merely my reaction to a very intimate portrait? Or was it something else, I thought, as I poured a dram of whisky.

The young woman's expression had been wistful, almost sad.

What was she thinking as she posed for La Geness? Something she had hoped for, that was not to be? Disappointment perhaps?

No, it was far stronger than disappointment. Sadness perhaps?

Nine

I RETURNED to the office on the Strand early in the morning, with thoughts of my next steps in attempting to learn more about Gwen Tavers's disappearance.

I was met at the sidewalk by Mr. Cavendish when I arrived.

"Have you spoken again with Mr. Tavers?" I inquired. "Has he received any word of his daughter?"

"I met him at the pub last night," he replied. "There's no word. And yerself?"

"Not as yet," I admitted. "However, there is someone I hope to meet with today in a related matter that might tell us something."

I was not willing to share more, as I knew all too well that it could only raise false hopes.

"And Mr. Brodie?" I then inquired.

"He did not return, and there's been no word from him. You know how it is when he's on a case for the Agency."

I did indeed, and he had been forthcoming that the inquiries he was following were indeed quite serious.

I was not unaware that there were 'distant rumblings,' as he called them, in affairs beyond England with the potential for far-reaching consequences. Bits and pieces of news regarding foreign difficulties were in the newspapers if one knew to look for them—the brief article regarding a cargo ship that had been seized, a foreign dignitary who had unexpectedly fallen ill, and the ever-present concerns over financial issues from the Continent.

My great-aunt, thought by some to be quite eccentric, kept a watchful eye regarding her own business interests there that included Mr. Munro. Especially regarding shipments of Old Lodge whisky and wine between Scotland and France.

I informed Mr. Cavendish that I would be working in the office and hoped to have an appointment in the afternoon.

"I will have messages that need to be sent by courier," I added as I bent to scratch Rupert behind the ears. His eyes closed with pleasure.

I chose to ignore the faint resemblance to Brodie in his reaction.

"I'll see to it, miss," Mr. Cavendish assured me. "I'll be at the Public House. Can I bring ye somethin' to eat?" he added with a wink.

He was as bad as Brodie when it came to teasing me about food.

"I'm certain the hound would appreciate that," I replied.

After all, I did share with him.

I unlocked the office door and paused as I stepped inside.

The office was much the same as usual—the smell of old places, of stone and wood and coal oil from the last fire in the iron stove, dust motes stirring just there in the light that came in through the window that looked out on the alleyway below. And shadows at the walls, the chalkboard, the bedroom beyond darkened.

"Bloody hell," I whispered to the empty office, absent Brodie at his desk pondering some note or one of my reports. No faint ring of fragrant pipe smoke encircling his head with that dark mane of hair, nor the way he looked up at me ...

"Best get on with it," I replied and turned on the electric that immediately banished the shadows.

I had my own desk with the portable typing machine he had purchased for me. I went to his desk instead. It did provide a better view of the chalkboard ...

I set my travel bag on the floor beside the desk, opened one of the drawers and took out note paper.

The first note to be delivered was to Mr. Dooley at New Scotland Yard, inquiring about any additional information in the Tavers or Davies inquiry cases. I closed, informing him that I could be reached either at the office or the townhouse.

The second message was for Mrs. Elizabeth Davies at their residence in Marylebone, since Mr. Harold Davies had been less than cooperative.

I was more than aware that she might refuse to meet with me, and informed her that I was presently making inquiries on another similar matter, and hoped to provide information for her family.

I paused before signing the note. I knew from Brodie that a polite request was easily turned down with an equally polite response, if any.

"A demand is different. It does not give the person a choice."

I was not of a mind to give Mrs. Davies a choice with an invitation that she could, and very likely would, refuse to accept.

I tore the note and tossed the pieces into the rubbish bin, then took out another piece of paper.

I wrote that I was making inquiries on behalf of a client

under similar circumstances and needed to meet with her to discuss her daughter's disappearance. I added that I would be at Slater's Tea Room in Piccadilly, at three o'clock that afternoon. It was not a request.

Slater's was favored by ladies of London for afternoon tea. I had only been there a time or two and had quickly escaped. I was not one for tea or gossip. However ...

It was located on the basement floor under the department store, and not at all a place where we might encounter Mr. Davies or anyone from the Foreign Office who might carry word back to him of my meeting with his wife.

I signed my name and enclosed one of the calling cards I recently had printed:

Brodie and Forsythe Private Investigations
#204 the Strand, London

There had been a conversation over that. He preferred 'Brodie and Brodie Private Investigations,' and had pointed out the fact that we were, after all, husband and wife.

I suspected at the time it was one of those peculiarities of men, particularly one who was a Scot, and pointed out there could be an advantage to having my own name on the card.

Most certainly when making inquiries on behalf of the royal family, whom I was acquainted with, as we had in one of our previous cases, and on behalf of female clients, who might be somewhat hesitant working with a man.

It was a small victory, but one nonetheless, as we encountered issues from time to time. I smiled as I tucked the note inside an envelope and delivered both messages to Mr. Cavendish.

"The courier is to wait for a response from Mr. Dooley once the note is delivered."

"I'll see to it straight away, miss," he assured me, then was on his way.

Upon returning to the office, I spent the next hour adding notes that I'd made the night before in my notebook, including the additional note that I intended to meet with Mrs. Davies.

I then went through the bills and letters that I'd pulled from the message box on the street. One envelope was quite thick from the Public Records Office.

Perhaps information Brodie was waiting for, I thought, and added it to the stack of mail on his desk.

There was still a good amount of time before departing for my meeting with Mrs. Davies. I returned to the sidewalk and purchased a copy of The Times morning edition from a boy on the street. I returned to the office and laid it across Brodie's desk, with that front page covered with personal advertisements.

The notices printed there didn't seem to be in any particular order with simple requests for someone's brother to contact his mother, mixed with more provocative advertisements for love, matrimony, or to meet—marital status not required.

From the information Mr. Charles in the advertising department had provided, the advertisement for #41984 was to run again today.

I eventually found it and circled it with my pen. Whoever had placed the advertisement apparently was still looking for that '*travel companion.*'

What of those who had already responded?

The service bell rang, jarring me from my thoughts.

Mr. Cavendish had returned.

"I delivered the notes to the courier service with instruction for him to wait for Mr. Dooley's answer."

He had also returned with luncheon from the Public House. The hound followed me up to the office. He was most appreciative to share the meal. He had absolutely no shame.

I arrived at Slater's before the appointed time and went downstairs to the tea room, where I asked for a table and gave the attendant my name. I informed him that I was waiting for someone to join me and requested a more private table.

I was shown to one under the arch of the stairs. It was set with white linen, the appropriate pieces for afternoon tea, and an arrangement of flowers.

As I waited, I did wonder if Mrs. Davies would arrive?

It was not unexpected under the circumstances that she might refuse. This was undoubtedly a difficult time for them, and perhaps there were others who claimed to be assisting with finding their daughter.

"Lady Forsythe?"

I looked up, the greeting quite hesitant.

"Mrs. Davies," I replied.

She nodded. "And this is my daughter, Rose. She insisted on accompanying me."

We sat across from one another with Rose beside her mother. She was a quiet, pensive girl who looked to be very near the same age as Lily was when she first arrived in London.

She listened to our conversation with a thoughtful expression, darting glances at her mother as Elizabeth Davies slowly removed her gloves.

She had brown hair and soft grey eyes. I saw in her the younger version in her daughter, Rose.

There was also an air of sadness along with the circles

beneath her eyes that no doubt was from the past several weeks, since the disappearance of her older daughter, Charlotte.

"Your note mentioned that you might be able to assist in finding my daughter."

Her voice quavered and I remembered the fear and the enormous control it had required for me to carry on when Linnie had disappeared two years before.

"Yes," I replied. "From my work on behalf of another client, there appear to be similarities and I hoped there might be something you could tell me about Charlotte's disappearance."

I then explained my inquiry on behalf of Reggie Tavers, although I did not go into specific details.

"The police..." Again her voice faltered. "My husband has made a report with them."

"They haven't provided any information," Rose added. "The answer is always the same when we inquire—they will notify us. Except they do not."

"Rose ..." her mother implored.

"I do not see any harm in telling her, if she can help."

"Mr. Davies has insisted that the police handle the matter," her mother went on to explain.

"I have contacted with him in the matter," I replied.

I saw no reason to hide the fact. He might speak of it eventually, even though he had refused to meet with me.

"I thought you might be able to provide information that could assist in the situation."

"The calling card you included? Brodie and Forsythe?" she inquired then.

"You resolved the murder attempt on the Prince of Wales!" Rose interjected.

"My husband and I assisted in the matter. Mr. Brodie was

previously with the Metropolitan Police for several years as inspector, now in private inquiries for clients.

"We have found that we are often able to assist in situations where some might be hesitant, or unable for whatever reason."

"It cannot hurt to have both doing whatever it takes to find Charlotte," Rose implored of her mother.

Mrs. Davies nodded. "I don't know what more I can tell you that we have not already told the police. But if you have questions, I will try to provide answers. I only want my daughter found, even though I know that with the amount of time that has passed ..." She removed a handkerchief from her reticule.

"I understand," I replied. "I have been through similar circumstances."

I left it at that, as our waiter returned with a fresh pot of tea and poured our cups. I waited until he departed. And then posed a question.

"Is there a young man in your daughter's life? A romantic attachment perhaps?"

"No," Mrs. Davies replied. "She is somewhat of an independent spirit, and spoke of remaining unattached for now."

"She wants to travel," Rose interjected. "She talked about Egypt and China all the time."

"A foolish notion," Mrs. Davies added. "We are not poor. Mr. Davies works very hard in his position. However, such ideas are simply not possible. It would cost a great deal, and we have Rose and her education to think of as well."

Her daughter frowned and made a sideways glance that said a great deal. It was something that I had seen from Lily, more than once. Not that I had never reacted in that same manner at their age ...

I thought of Lizzie Smith and her postcards.

"Did she collect pictures of any of those places? Was she perhaps saving for those travels?"

"We provide the girls everything they need. Any money they have would be gifts from family."

"She wanted to take a position," Rose added, which brought a startled look from her mother.

"There are not many opportunities for respectable young ladies," Mrs. Davies added.

Unless they created those opportunities for themselves. I thought of my novels that were published. Might Charlotte Davies have been motivated to that sort of thing, or some other means of earning money for the travels she wanted to make?

"She answered an advertisement in the newspaper," Rose commented.

Her mother turned to her. "What advertisement? Your sister said nothing of this to me."

"It's found on the first page of The Times. It mentioned a travel companion and all expenses paid."

Rose was certainly far more well-informed than her mother.

"She showed it to me and said that she was going to reply to it. I warned her that you wouldn't be pleased," she told her mother. "But she was very determined."

Elizabeth Davies stared at her younger daughter.

"And you said nothing about this."

"She knew you would disapprove, and made me promise that I wouldn't say anything."

"Did she receive a response?" I asked. "Something that would have been posted in the paper?"

Rose nodded. "She received instructions through the same box number where she was to meet the person who placed it.

She was so excited. It seemed like a wonderful opportunity for her to travel."

And she had not returned.

"You spoke of a similar situation."

I looked over at Rose.

"My sister disappeared." I didn't mention that her maid was found murdered.

"Did it ... end well?" she asked.

I assured her that it had.

"Then there is still hope ... that she might be found."

I assured her that there was. There was no need at this point to explain the horrifying statistics about young women across London who disappeared all the time, and were never found. It was a sad, tragic part of our inquiry business.

She reached across and took hold of my hand "You must tell me when you find anything that might tell us what has happened."

I told her that I would.

"You've been very helpful. I will contact you when I learn something important."

I thanked Rose as well. "I realize that you made a promise to Charlotte—however, you did the right thing telling me about the advertisement."

I watched as Mrs. Davies and Rose departed the tea room.

These situations were always difficult, and I felt enormously sad for their family.

Brodie had warned me, there were times when the inquiry business was often heartbreaking.

Yet I was determined to find answers for Mr. and Mrs. Davies and Reggie Tavers.

After leaving Rose and her mother, I returned to the office on the Strand to update my notes and also to send round a message to Mr. Dooley at New Scotland Yard about the additional information I had learned regarding the disappearance of Charlotte Davies.

"There was a message sent round for you, miss," Mr. Cavendish informed me. He handed me an envelope.

It was from Monsieur La Geness according to the name across the back of the envelope.

"And Mr. Dooley was just here not more than an hour past," Mr. Cavendish added. "He said you was to contact him straight away at the Bond Street station."

"Did he say what it was about?"

"Only that it was important."

I tucked the envelope from La Geness into my travel bag and waved down a cab.

It had grown quite late, street lamps well-lit as I arrived at the Bond Street Station, with the hound at Mr. Cavendish's insistence. He trotted alongside as I entered the station. I went directly to the desk sergeant and informed him that Mr. Dooley was expecting me. He appeared almost immediately.

Mr. Dooley had once served under Brodie when he was with the MET, and had made detective the year before. He had provided valuable information to us on more than one occasion, even when it was against the policy of the Metropolitan Police.

In spite of the difficult circumstances that led to Brodie's departure from the MET, I was aware that he held a deep respect for Brodie from their time together.

He was somewhat short of stature, barely taller than myself, with a ruddy complexion, sandy hair, and a direct gaze that now fastened on me. He took me by the arm and directed me to a small room that was much like others among the police stations where people were taken for questioning in the matter of a crime.

"What is it?" I asked as I took a chair beside the small desk.

He closed the door. "I learned of it right after I received yer message, and thought it best to speak with you first. Mr. Brodie is not with you?"

"He has not returned as yet."

He nodded, his expression quite grim. "It seemed important to send round a note considerin' the two other cases," he explained.

"You must tell me what has happened, Mr. Dooley," I insisted.

"A young woman's body has been found."

Ten

"WHERE?" I asked.

"Southwark, near the river. At least what was left of her," Mr. Dooley replied. "The body has been taken to Kew."

Kew Mortuary was where bodies were now taken and held over until they could be identified.

According to what Brodie had shared, very often no one stepped forward to claim the bodies that were found in the Thames. Either due to lack of money for a proper burial, or out of fear that they might be accused of the crime of murder.

Under more horrific circumstances, bodies in the past had been disposed of in the river after being sold to the medical society for dissection and study.

"I want to see it."

"Not a pretty sight when the river and other things have been at them. Mr. Brodie might not approve you goin' there."

"Nevertheless, Mr. Dooley. I would very much appreciate it if you could arrange it. It could be important to our client."

He nodded. "Wait here, miss. I'll place a telephone call and let them know we'll be round."

An ache had begun at the back of my head as I sat and waited with Rupert. He lay at my feet, brown eyes staring up at me.

Even though Mr. Dooley returned in short order, I was still impatient even though such things were never pleasant. And it was not as if I hadn't seen a body before. In fact, I had seen more than one in the course of working with Brodie.

What would I find when I accompanied Mr. Dooley? It could be a fool's errand—bodies appeared frequently across London. Still ... it was important that I know.

He returned in short order. "I have a driver waiting."

He escorted us from the station to a waiting coach, the hound trotting at my heel.

Rupert jumped in after me as Mr. Dooley gave the driver, in police uniform, our destination.

The Kew Mortuary was in Richmond, a lengthy ride across London. Not that I wasn't familiar with Richmond. An acquaintance owned several boats on the Richmond canal.

He had retired from the sea after losing his leg in one of the accidents that were quite common aboard ship. He had traded a merchantman that regularly made the voyage from London to India, for the smaller canal boats, his cargo traded for passengers who ventured into the countryside beyond the city, then returning with fresh produce for London markets.

Linnie and I had first made the acquaintance of Captain Turner on one of those canal voyages to riverside villages and farms. More recently he provided information regarding certain cargos that were received at the London Docks through old friends from his days aboard the merchantmen and schooners. But this was hardly a trip for pleasure into the countryside.

It was early evening when we arrived at Kew, a single lamp

burning beside a small block building attached to the back of a larger building just east of the Kew Bridge.

Just beyond that large building a line of trees was outlined against the night sky filled with a grey hue from the northern lights that cast a melancholy gloom over the countryside.

Mr. Dooley assisted me down from the coach. He ordered the driver to wait. I gave the hound instructions to 'stay' in the coach. Mr. Dooley then escorted me toward that single light at the entrance to the mortuary.

I have discovered that there are sights and smells that once experienced, are never forgotten. They were there now as an attendant answered the bell-pull at the door. He nodded to Mr. Dooley and then escorted us inside.

The mortuary was spartan and stark with concrete block walls, a single light overhead, and the attendant's desk. A door beyond led inside the holding area.

Mr. Dooley nodded to the attendant, signed a log book, and we were then shown into the main part of Kew Mortuary.

I had seen the inside of such places before, with several rooms, each with lights, stark white walls and tables, with rolling trays of physician's instruments. At the Bow Street Station, there were holding rooms with what were referred to as 'cold' boxes, compartments with blocks of ice that lined the wall where bodies were stored until identification could be made.

That stark accommodation would be considered extravagant compared to what I saw now.

This, as Mr. Dooley had explained, was the final place a body was taken if it was not identified, only to then be buried in an anonymous grave in a graveyard nearby.

The hallway that led into that larger room was dimly lit. It was impossible to see what waited in that larger room until I stepped into it.

"Over here." The attendant indicated a table with a sheet draped over what appeared to be a small body.

"Are ye certain that you're up to this, miss?" Mr. Dooley again inquired.

I nodded. It hardly seemed that whatever was under that sheet could be an adult person, but he had assured me that it was a young woman.

"Please continue, Mr. Dooley."

He nodded to the attendant and he drew the sheet back.

I heard a sudden gasp and realized that it was my own as I stared at the body—or what remained of it on that table, and realized the reason it had seemed smaller than expected.

Both legs were missing as well as one arm and a good portion of the other, leaving hardly more than the young woman's torso.

"Are you all right, Miss?"

I realized then that Mr. Dooley was holding onto my arm. I took a deep breath and nodded.

"Do you recognize her?" he asked.

I forced myself to look past the severed places where her arms and legs had been, and stepped closer under the light fixture.

I nodded. "Yes."

The young woman's hair was matted and tangled with all sort of debris. Wherever she had been, whatever had happened, the evidence of it was there. Only the remnants of clothes remained, stained with blood and grime. Her features were battered and bruised.

One eye was swollen shut, the other, dark brown, stared up at the ceiling. Yet, beneath the grim bruises and blood, there was a person. A young woman I did recognize in spite of all of it—Lizzie Smith, the young woman who sold flowers at Covent Garden.

I recognized her from that photograph of two young women, smiling for the photographer, both with hopes and dreams of travel.

I returned to Bond Street with Mr. Dooley, where I made a statement about Lizzie Smith, how I knew of her and then gave him the name of the other young woman in the photograph—Gwen Tavers.

"I'll put some men on it first thing in the mornin', now that we know who she was," he said gently. "And I'll check with the boys who work the streets out of the station house nearest Southwark. At least we know the poor thing's name. But with no family ..."

I already knew what he was going to say. There was no one to collect the body, no one to mourn her. Except perhaps for a young man at Covent Garden.

Only more questions.

Who would do such a thing to a young woman? What had happened? Where was she the past days after she disappeared? Had she answered that advertisement for a travel companion? And then met with someone?

If so, who had placed that advertisement with The Times?

I had given my word to Reggie Tavers that I would help find his daughter. And now possibly Charlotte Davies as well. I knew as well as anyone, perhaps more so, the fear and heartache one went through when someone they loved disappeared.

I was struggling with all of it. With the gruesome sight of what remained of that poor girl's body, that brought back memories of my sister's maid.

Brodie had told me that it would always be there.

And two other young women were still missing. Was that to be their fate as well?

This was far more than a young woman's desire for travel and adventure that had gotten her into some mischief.

So many questions with no answers. And only one clue that connected them—that advertisement in the newspaper.

I needed Brodie, to tell him about Lizzie Smith, and ask what was to be done.

"Lady Forsythe?"

Mr. Dooley, kind and caring. I looked over at him.

"How do you do this day after day?" I asked.

"I think of my Maeve and the young ones," he replied. "It's all that's needed to start the next day."

His wife and children, with the hope of protecting them, and others. Very much like Brodie.

He was quiet as he assisted me into the coach.

"I'll see you home."

It was late when we arrived at Mayfair, the ride silent, Rupert with his head on my knee as if he sensed the tragedy.

Mr. Dooley escorted me to the door and waited as I found the key.

Mrs. Ryan was there.

"I'll be sayin' good night then, miss." He tipped his hat and returned to the coach.

"I held supper over ..." Mrs. Ryan said then stopped.

Whatever else she might have said was set aside, usually a comment about Rupert. But the frown on her face was not for him. Her hand was warm and comforting on my cold one.

"Come along, miss," she said gently, without the usual Irish fire in her voice. "And that scraggly animal as well."

· · ·

I didn't sleep. It was impossible with images of poor Lizzie Smith there each time I closed my eyes.

I eventually rose and dressed for the day, even though it was only half past four of the morning.

The hound was there, as he had been through the long hours of the night, standing guard, or more accurately snoring on the floor beside the bed. He looked up at me somewhat anxiously.

"I'll let you out," I told him. "Mrs. Ryan will not be pleased if you soil the carpets."

Brodie would have simply shaken his head at that—talking to Rupert as if he understood.

I was convinced that he did as he led the way down the stairs and to the front entrance, made a somewhat desperate sound, and then bounded down the steps with some urgency.

I returned to the parlor and spent the next hour making notes in my notebook about the night before. I then read back over everything I had written after meeting with Reggie Tavers.

I heard sounds from the kitchen. Mrs. Ryan was up and about as well, as was her usual habit. Knowing me quite well, she brought steaming hot coffee and biscuits into the parlor and set the tray on the desk. Also, knowing me quite well, there were no questions about the previous evening.

I added new questions to my notebook, then sat staring at them for some time. I looked over at the nudge of a nose against my knee.

Rupert had returned, and Mrs. Ryan with him. She stood at the entrance to the parlor.

"He came round to the service entrance ... with this."

She held a parcel in her hands, somewhat the worse for wear. At least it was not something thoroughly disgusting.

"There's an address," she added. "Mrs. Ponsonby, at Number 20, down the way."

The expression on the hound's face—Brodie insisted there was no such thing as an animal having an expression—was quite innocent.

"I'll see that it's returned," she added. "Will you be wantin' breakfast, Miss Mikaela?"

"No, I'll be leaving shortly."

I could do nothing here, and perhaps there was some word from Brodie.

I put the notebook into my travel bag, and gave Rupert a biscuit.

"You'll spoil the animal."

I looked down at him, the biscuit thoroughly consumed. He grinned at me. I very much needed that. I gave him the last one and called for a cab.

There was something to be said for morning traffic through London, usually muttered with a curse or two by most who were caught in the congestion.

The City of London had announced plans for the expansion of the underground rail system in partnership with the rail companies, that would greatly relieve the congestion. However …

As with most things, progress was quite slow. At present there were only articles in the dailies about the open trenches under main thoroughfares that only added congestion to streets that were already almost impassable as we came to another stop.

I had the driver stop as we were quite near the Strand. I paid him, and Rupert and I continued afoot.

"Mornin', miss," Mr. Cavendish greeted me as we arrived at the office.

"I was fairly certain the lad was with you when he didn't show at the Public House or here for supper."

"Has Mr. Brodie returned?" I asked with a glance up to the second-floor landing and saw the still-darkened window.

"Or perhaps some word from him?"

He shook his head. "There's been none, miss."

I made no attempt to hide my disappointment. "You will let me know immediately if there is a message?"

"Of course, miss."

Before he could ask if there was anything new regarding my inquiries for Gwen Tavers, I quickly continued up the stairs.

The office was as it had been the day before, as I entered, crossed to the window that looked over the alley, and raised the shade, then set my bag on Brodie's desk.

Very well. I would add my notes to the board, then place a call to Mr. Dooley at the Yard for any word from the men with the MET who worked in the district nearest Southwark—although I was aware that there were not regular patrols by constables in most of the outlying areas. Brodie had spoken of it, and apparently little had changed since his time with the Metropolitan Police.

Mr. Dooley was not available, nor was Brodie with my inquiry at the Agency. I asked to speak with Alex Sinclair, whom we had both worked with in the past.

He was quite young, but brilliant, and always coming up with a new invention such as his coding machine, and some sort of tracking device with a small built-in timepiece that responded to a battery-operated hand-held mechanism.

There had been some missteps there, and he had been quite busy the past six months making improvements.

I explained that I needed to speak with Brodie. However,

he had not seen him the past two days. Or that was possibly what he was supposed to tell anyone who inquired.

It was as if Brodie had disappeared ... I looked again at the notes I'd made on the board. There was someone who might know where he was ...

I grabbed my bag, locked the office, and had Mr. Cavendish wave down a driver.

Mr. Symons greeted me at the entrance as I arrived at Sussex Square.

"Mikaela! How very splendid, my dear," Aunt Antonia emerged from the small parlor, wearing a bright-green dressing gown and a turban.

"You may join us for brunch. Then after, I'm instructing Lily in the finer strategies of baccarat."

Gambling. Most definitely something she might need, I thought.

"Is Munro about?" I asked.

"Mr. Munro? I'm not certain."

"I heard Mrs. Roberts in the kitchen say that he returned late last night." Lily had joined us.

"If so, he is undoubtedly in the wine cellar, dear," my great-aunt added.

The wine cellar was an expansion of the original dungeons at Sussex Square. They had been walled off when it was determined that the smaller, cramped cells from our ancestors' time would hardly accommodate supplies, machinery for the water system, nor the kegs of heating oil for the countless lamps that lit the estate.

The need for a larger space had only increased with my great-aunt's venture into the whisky and wine trade, with barrels and kegs stored there. The cellar had also provided far easier access to the kitchens on the main floor.

I had been down in the cellar previously. I could have taken the lift that had been installed for ease when taking things up to the kitchens ... however, the stairs were much quicker. I called out as I reached the stone floor.

The cellar was well lit by electric lights on the ceiling that illuminated rows of casks and barrels, all meticulously logged and accounted for, as well as crates of fabrics and wood boxes that contained all manner of china and silver pieces, along with furnishings that were stored there.

It had once been a hodgepodge of accumulation over the centuries. When Munro joined the household, the first thing he did was to organize all of it. Aunt Antonia claimed that he knew where each and every piece was. A slight exaggeration, I thought.

A resident cat that lived in the cellar suddenly darted from among stacked barrels, along with a long shadow as Munro stepped into the light from the overhead fixture.

He was very near as tall as Brodie, with that same leanness from years together as boys on the streets of Edinburgh.

I had heard some of the stories from Brodie, others he simply shook his head when I asked a question.

"It is not for you, lass."

The two were very near the same age, though there was no certainty of either one. He had been the first one on the street, who took on a lanky boy as companion in their schemes, and then travelled together to London.

His hair was dark as Brodie's, worn long much the same, but there were lines at the corners of his eyes that told more of the story of their hard youth, with a faint scar or two among them. Strikingly handsome some might say. I would say dangerous.

It was his eyes, a piercing shade of blue that had the ability to stop a person cold with a single look. If they were wise enough. That gaze fastened on me now.

The streets had hardened him, to be certain. It was there now in the set of his shoulders, the wary stance that slowly relaxed as he saw me.

"Miss Mikaela."

Wherever he had been before returning to Sussex Square, the shadow was still there. Hard things that men didn't speak of.

"What brings ye to Sussex Square?" That Scots accent, still there after all the years since, slipped through as it did with Brodie when he was lost in thought or there was some difficulty.

"I need to speak with you about an inquiry case I've taken."

We sat at the small round table that was nothing more than an overturned oak wine barrel where he worked on his accounting log for supplies at Sussex Square, and I explained what I knew, and what had happened.

He listened in that quiet way so very much like Brodie, and I could only imagine the lives of two boys as they listened at doors, slipped down alleyways, stole from a vendor's cart, then slipped silently away into the night.

He continued to listen when I told him about the advertisement that all three young women had apparently responded to, then the trip to Kew Mortuary with Mr. Dooley the previous evening.

"It is more than a young girl simply taking herself off for a stay-over with a friend for a bit of adventure. Two other young women responded to that advertisement and are now missing. There may be more."

"Ye shouldn't have gone with Mr. Dooley."

"Nevertheless, I cannot ignore what has happened or the possible danger to others. Do you know where Brodie is? If I could speak with him ..."

He shook his head. "Only that it was a matter for the Agency. Ye'd best leave it to Mr. Dooley until Brodie returns. He'll help as he can then, goin' to those he knows to help find the women."

He hadn't answered that question—where Brodie was. Another stubborn Scot. I rose from my chair.

"By then, it might be too late."

"Wait for him to return, Miss Mikaela," he cautioned again.

I didn't remain for luncheon. I had no appetite, something most unusual for me.

Instead, I returned to the office on the Strand.

I spent the next few hours studying the notes I'd made at the chalkboard.

Lizzie Smith was dead. What of Gwen Tavers and Charlotte Davies?

I sat at Brodie's desk and went back to the front page of the newspaper from the day before, with those Personals advertisements.

'Seeking female companion for same, for travel and adventure. Age 18-25. All expenses paid. No whores or prostitutes need reply. Respond #41984.'

I took out my pen and a piece of notepaper. I kept the note simple:

'*I am a respectable girl of the age required.*
I am a hard worker and wish to travel.'

I didn't sign my name, but instead added, *'Waiting for your reply.'* I then put it in an envelope, sealed it, and wrote that box number on the outside.

I hesitated. I went back over everything I'd learned, everything on the board. I closed my eyes in an attempt to forget what I had seen at Kew. But it was still there.

"I need this delivered to The Times newspaper advertising department," I told Mr. Cavendish when I reached the bottom of the stairs.

"It is important and must be delivered straight away."

Eleven

THE NEXT DAY ...

I WAITED for the morning issue of The Times.

There was no guarantee that I would receive a response, yet I felt compelled to send a reply to the advertisement.

If I could not find who was behind those advertisements and another young woman might die.

I had learned from Brodie early on in our inquiry partnership that there is no such thing as coincidence, or random crimes. Each has a purpose and a person behind it.

What sort of person was behind the murder of an innocent flower seller? I knew the obvious reason, of course. The crime sheets of the dailies were filled with the assaults on girls and women in the East End. 'A plague of predators,' one report had called it. An innocent person in the wrong place at the wrong time ...

Yet, this was different, and somehow even more terrifying. I refused to believe that it was a random assault on a street corner or in a tavern. From the little I knew about Lizzie Smith, she was not that sort.

She was hard-working, and a dreamer at the same time, who longed to leave the Garden behind and travel.

A tragic accident? The condition of Lizzie Smith's body did not speak to an accident. As Inspector Dooley pointed out afterward, the condition of her body had been deliberate, with but one purpose—so that she would not easily be found nor the individual who had murdered her discovered.

Deliberate. It was the only word for what had happened to Lizzie Smith. And with two additional missing young women, it was possible that it would happen again.

I had put in a telephone call to the Agency through the woman who insisted there was no phone connection, until I gave her a specific calling number for the Scientific Development Department, where Alex Sinclair worked on his latest inventions.

"Lady Forsythe?" he remarked with some surprise. "How is it that you were able to put through the call?" He paused. "Do not tell me. I do not want to know. It undoubtedly has to do with a certain member of the royal family. "

I did not tell him. Instead, I insisted that I needed to speak with Brodie. There was another pause at the other end of the call.

"The official response is that I do not know where he is."

The official response? Of course, that meant that he knew very well where Brodie was, or in the least had the ability to contact him.

I liked Alex very much. He was charming in that way of someone who is perpetually distracted, his mind always on one of his inventions. He was highly intelligent, and we had shared more than one inquiry case.

I remained calm but insistent when I informed him that the matter was most urgent, that Brodie was aware of the case, that I valued his loyalty and talents, and did not believe him for a minute that he didn't know where Brodie might be found.

He repeated that official response. Most aggravating.

"When you *do not* see him next or *do not* know where he is," I replied, "you must tell him that I need to speak with him." And added that it was most important.

Official response, indeed!

Short of being able to reach Brodie, I did hope was that Munro might be able to find him.

I waited through the remainder of the day until the evening issue of the newspaper appeared on the street, and quickly scanned the Personals advertisements on the front page. The original advertisement was there, but there was no response.

I was convinced that it had been foolish on my part, to think that it would appear that quickly ... if at all.

Perhaps I had not seemed eager enough in my response, or perhaps it was off-putting for some reason. Or ... there was a possibility that several other young women had replied, mine merely one among several.

When the morning of the second day arrived and there was still no answer, I returned to Sussex Square. However, Munro was not there.

I returned to the office on the Strand much to Lily's protest, and went over everything I had learned since taking up the case for Reggie Tavers.

There had to be something that I was missing, some piece of information I had overlooked or thought unimportant.

I was not usually one given to outbursts of frustration. Anger was one thing, however I was usually calm and quite rational when it came to deciphering information.

"Yer not one to throw a *wobbly* and go off into one about something like most women I know," Brodie once said.

Of course that led to a bit of a conversation about the women he did know.

It was the ringing of the service bell that pulled me back to the matter at hand. I immediately went out onto the landing.

"The evening paper, miss." Mr. Cavendish held it aloft.

I had asked him to watch for the news boys who appeared on the street when each new issue came out. I ran down the stairs to the sidewalk.

He handed me the newspaper.

I was not one to spend hours each day idly reading about the latest crimes in London, the society pages with the announcements of the forthcoming soirees, who was seen with whom, or those Personals advertisements.

"Is there somethin' the matter, miss? Somethin' I can help you with?"

I thanked him but I couldn't tell him about Lizzie Smith and what I had seen, nor what it might mean for Reggie Tavers's daughter.

I made an excuse and quickly returned to the office.

I laid the newspaper out on Brodie's desk and quickly found that original advertisement ... And below it the response to my inquiry!

'Respectable Girl. We must meet.
3:00
18-Jun.
#4 Princes Gate, Knightsbridge'

I sat back in the chair. A time, and a location.

I had hoped but held no confidence that there would be a response.

The message stared back at me. The following day was the

18th of June, and I was to be there at three o'clock in the afternoon.

What would I find when I arrived there?

I was not familiar with the address, yet there was an establishment that would know. I folded the newspaper and tucked it inside my travel bag, then locked the office door.

Mr. Cavendish was not about, nor the hound. I waved down a cab and gave the driver the location of the courier office.

The office was well lit when I arrived, as they remained open for late customers.

"That address would be in Knightsbridge," the attendant behind the desk informed me. "That would be Kilburn House, according to our records. It's been marked off for deliveries for some time in the records we receive from the postal office.

"Could be that no one lives there anymore."

That made no sense. Or, very possibly it made perfect sense, for someone who was determined to remain anonymous.

I returned to the Strand. I had a great deal to think about.

I spent the night at the office on the Strand with Rupert on the floor beside the bed. It was a restless night and I finally rose very near five in the morning, dressed, then went out into the office.

As the hour grew later, there was still no word from Brodie, and I made a plan.

I could not, would not abandon the only chance I might have to find Gwen Tavers and Charlotte Davies. Whatever had happened to them, I was convinced it was connected to the disappearance of Lizzie Smith.

However, I was not naïve. I was planning on entering into what might prove a very dangerous situation. Therefore, I sat down at Brodie's desk and took several steps prior to setting off for that address in Knightsbridge.

I made a telephone call to the Yard, and was informed that Inspector Dooley was not available. I then wrote out a message for Brodie for the courier service to deliver to the Agency at the Tower, with no way of knowing when he might receive it.

That done, I went to the board, and went over everything I had written, searching for anything that might tell me more. I then prepared for my meeting with the person who had replied to my response.

I had chosen my clothes carefully. I wore a simple worsted walking skirt with a shirtwaist and scuffed boots that I kept at the office. Much the same that a *respectable girl* might wear who hoped to secure the position that had been advertised.

My hair was pinned up under a simple boat hat, and I carried my travel bag as though I hoped to immediately set off on the adventure that had been promised in that advertisement.

Yet, inside that bag, along with my notebook and that newspaper ad response, were the revolver Brodie insisted I always carry, along with the knife Mr. Munro had given me.

I had allowed myself a full hour with the usual traffic to make the ride from the office.

Mr. Cavendish was there at the sidewalk and I asked him to wave down a driver.

"It's late in the day. Mr. Brodie wouldn't have ye go by yerself," Mr. Cavendish reminded me.

"Nevertheless," I replied.

He frowned, shook his head, then gave off a shrill whistle and the hound popped out of the alcove.

I had no idea what I might find in Knightsbridge; however,

it was very likely the hound would not be well received. Still, I would not argue the matter with Mr. Cavendish.

I stepped into the cab. The hound jumped in after.

As we left the Strand, I had the driver stop. The hound might very well draw suspicion from whomever was at that address in Knightsbridge, and even though I regretted setting him off, I was convinced it was necessary.

"Home!" I told him, one of the words I had been teaching him.

He stared up at me from the street with a confused expression. I then had the driver continue on.

Even with the late afternoon traffic that often brought the main streets in London to a stop, we arrived in Knightsbridge in a timely manner.

"Princes Gate?" the driver announced with some doubt as he pulled the cab to a stop at the corner.

"Are ye sure, miss?"

I caught the uncertainty in his voice. It matched my own.

I was somewhat familiar with the area surrounding Knightsbridge from several years before, but not this part, which had once been an area of stately manors that were now dark and abandoned with only a single streetlamp, in a part of London where there was not yet any electric.

I thought of the information the attendant at the courier office had given me, that there had been no deliveries for quite a while.

"It is the address I was given," I told the driver and asked him to continue on.

We reached the next street and he turned the rig then stopped.

"Number 4, Princes Gate, miss," he called down.

Number 4 was an enormous Georgian manor, surrounded

by cut-stone walls with a double wrought-iron gate overgrown with vines under overhanging tree limbs.

The exterior of the manor was of brick and stone, a once elegant residence that was in disrepair, with rusted frames around sash windows at the first- and second-story rooms, the glass smeared and caked with seasons of neglect.

"Don't look like there's anyone about," the driver commented.

In the fading light of day, I had to agree. Had I been sent on a fool's errand?

There was only one way to find out. I stepped down from the cab.

"Please wait," I told the driver and paid him an extra amount for the additional time. Knightsbridge was a good distance from the Strand and even farther from Mayfair. If no one answered the door, then I had a good walk before I might find another driver if he were to leave.

I crossed Princes Gate to that wrought-iron entrance. The gate creaked loudly as I pushed it open then continued on that stone walkway to the main entrance.

A bell cord hung beside a door carved with animals but now faded, the wood splintered with neglect.

I pulled the cord.

There was a distant sound from somewhere inside. When there was no answer, I pulled on the bell pull a second time.

There was still no answer. I then knocked on the door. To my surprise, it slowly opened.

I hesitated. There was no one at the entrance. Had someone departed and not latched the door securely? Or was it that the latch was simply badly worn?

I had not come all this way to turn around and leave. I thought of the revolver in my bag, then decided against it as it could be frightening for others. I stepped inside the entrance hall.

It was long and narrow, with a faded tapestry on one wall and an overstuffed head of a bear with bared teeth that loomed up out of the shadows at the opposite wall, and led to a room on the right with a set of double doors that stood open.

In the fading light that spilled into the hall from glass panels at that front entrance it appeared to be a drawing room with furnishings draped with cloths, and a large fireplace with a wood mantel decorated with carvings of dogs.

I called out as I returned to the hall and had almost decided that the response in the newspaper had been nothing more than some deception by whoever placed the ad when I heard the sound of movement behind me.

"Hello?" I called again as I turned.

The blow was sudden, painful, and I felt myself going down ...

I wakened slowly and winced at the pain in the back of my head as the room gradually settled into place and I slowly sat up. However, I was not in the room with those dogs on the elaborately carved mantel.

It appeared to be a bedroom, with faded, heavy satin drapes on the windows, the settee on which I sat, and a scarred but once impressive mahogany washstand with a porcelain basin.

I heard nothing, saw no one. All I could think was that very likely Charlotte Davies and Gwen Tavers might very well have been lured here the same way and then experienced the same greeting.

Then the question, where were they? Along with whoever

had given me that bump on the head and then brought me to that room?

And what did they have planned next?

I searched for my travel bag but it was gone, no doubt taken by the person who delivered that blow.

I sat up on the settee, the fabric faded and torn in the light from a single candle, and crossed the room to the door. It was locked, not unexpected I supposed, all things considered.

Several thoughts raced through my head. The manor obviously was not completely abandoned. Someone had taken it upon himself to welcome me in a most unwelcome manner.

From experience it was not lost on me that the 'welcome,' as I called it, could well have been far more than a bump on the head. It was safe to assume that whoever had attacked me did not intend to seriously harm me, or some other fate that often befell a woman out and about on her own in parts of London.

I thought fleetingly of the hound. The situation might have been far different if I had allowed him to accompany me. However ...

I went to the windows. Equally smudged and neglected, they faced out to the street below where I had left my driver.

I had no way of knowing how long I had been out, however the street beyond was quite dark, my driver nowhere in sight. It did appear that I was on my own.

I reached down and removed the slender pick from the inside of my boot then returned to the door.

Given the approximate age of the house, the lock was equally old and not easily persuaded. However, with patience and with what Brodie had taught me, I slowly turned the pick and listened for the distinctive sound of metal on the iron lever. A second attempt was necessary as I eased the pick under the lever inside once more and slowly eased it up. The lock opened.

I listened for any sound beyond the door.

There was none and I eased it open and discovered an empty hallway.

I have been in old buildings before, but those were more often tenements or rundown flats where our inquiry cases had taken us.

The manor was at least two hundred years old, and although in much neglect, it had a series of rooms behind other closed doors on the second floor that I had viewed from the street.

The walls in the hallway were covered with murals, paintings, and several stuffed deer heads that looked down on me as I carefully made my way down the length of the hall. I passed an ornate Ormolu clock covered with several layers of dust, and a marble bust that appeared to be a young Duke of Wellington with a sword. With my bag confiscated, I picked up the sword.

In spite of the dust, obvious neglect, and the decay of the manor, it was obvious that someone lived here by the nasty bump on the back of my head.

But who? And where were they?

I tried one door and discovered it was also locked. There was no sound from within the room, nor from the locked room across the hall.

I reached the center of that hallway, dimly lit by gas lights on the walls that cast an eerie shadow over everything. There were windows at the near end of the second floor of the manor, and I discovered a wide stairway with ornate carved wood bannisters, once quite beautiful, now dull and darkened over time.

I pressed myself against the wall at a sound from the floor below. It came again, along with the faint light that flickered from a candle or possibly an oil lantern.

I refused to go back to that room, and glanced to the stairs that obviously led to the third floor. As that light grew nearer, I quickly made my decision and climbed the stairs.

They widened at that upper floor, the landing leading to a set of double doors.

A ballroom, or great hall? It made no sense that it was on the third floor where guests would have to pass through the other two floors of sitting rooms and bedrooms below.

Possibly a trophy room, considering those stuffed animal heads I had seen? Or an enormous game room?

I went to those doors and listened. When no sound came from within, I tried the lever. The doors were not locked. I pushed one door open and stepped inside.

It was neither a ballroom or great hall. Nor a trophy room. Unless what I glimpsed in the flickering light of candles were the trophies ...

There were at least a half dozen portraits in that same provocative style I had seen at the Grosvenor Gallery. Yet, it was more than that.

Two of the portraits seemed very near complete, and I recognized the young woman in each one—Gwen Tavers with Lizzie Smith! The resemblance was unmistakable.

The third portrait? It too had recently been started, but was far from complete. Still the resemblance was near enough to her younger sister that I knew for certain it had to be Charlotte Davies!

And a fourth one, barely more than sketches that the artist had begun to fill in. It was of a young woman barely dressed in a deep red gown, as if she had been discovered as she undressed, the length of her back naked as she turned and looked over her shoulder.

The artist had just begun to fill out her features—the arch

of dark brows, the deep red hair that spilled over her shoulder and down her back, and that dark crimson gown.

I stared in horror as I recognized myself!

"I am always making sketches ..."

"I hadn't anticipated it, of course. But now that you are here ... Magnificent!"

A voice behind me, one that I had heard before—articulate, yet soft-spoken, with that faint accent giving compliments when we met. I slowly turned.

Simon La Geness, whose portraits at the Grosvenor had drawn curiosity, comments, acclaim, and no small amount of criticism for their provocative, barely clothed subjects.

"What is this?" I asked, in an effort to understand what I was looking at. And the other portraits ...

"Lady Forsythe, and I must admit unexpected. But now that you are here ..."

That faint smile.

"So much more than I could have hoped for. Yet, I should have known. Most particularly when I learned of your reputation with your inquiry cases." He slowly walked toward me, though it seemed with some difficulty, that smile disappearing with the effort.

"I will admit, the fascination was there. You are quite beautiful with a strength and something else that needed very much to be put on canvas—something almost secretive. Who would have thought that you would provide the opportunity?"

What was he talking about?

"Of course, you will be the centerpiece of the collection," he announced.

He must be mad. It was the only word to describe what I was hearing. What of Lizzie Smith? Her portrait was there along with the others.

"Why?" But I knew even as I asked the question. That advertisement—*Seeking female companion for travel and adventure.*

There was no travel in it, and the only adventure appeared to be ...

My head ached as it all slowly came together.

"You cannot hope to keep this secret," I told him. "Where are the others? What about Lizzie Smith?"

"Most unfortunate about the girl," he replied with a noticeable quaver at his voice. Regret? Remorse?

"She chose to leave. Although the others are here," he assured me, yet in a voice that was quite odd and chilling.

Chose to leave? His way of describing that he had her killed?

And the other young women? Had they met the same fate as Lizzie Smith?

"Where are they?" I demanded.

"All in due time ... if you cooperate," he replied as he slowly came closer.

I raised the sword.

"*Maitenant tu fais quoi.* What will you do now?" he repeated in English. "If you kill me, you kill them as well."

Kill them as well? What was he talking about? Were they in danger even as we spoke?

I hesitated. In that moment, I wanted very much to run him through for that smile, the arrogance, the insanity in what he was telling me. Or in the very least to wound him and then find the other women.

He must be insane. It was the only possible answer.

Yet, the threat was real. One young woman, Lizzie Smith, was already dead.

Hadn't I seen it before, that search for my sister, the

madness that gleamed in the eyes of another where no amount of reason or persuasion might reach them.

Brodie had spoken of it from his own experience as he explained that moment, that look in another person's eyes where nothing that was said could persuade them against what they had set out to do.

I couldn't risk endangering the others, and slowly lowered the saber ...

Twelve

BRODIE READ THE TELEGRAM AGAIN, then cursed. It was two bloody days old!

Held for him by the owner at the inn. Two days since that message had been sent, when he knew from experience that hours were often the difference between life and … He refused to think of the possibility as he read it again:

'Urgent. M's inquiry case, now a murder.
She's disappeared. Munro.'

And the worst of it, there was nothing from Mikaela. No telegram. Nothing.

"What is it, my friend?" Herr Schmidt inquired, his blunt features heavily lined from the past several days that had taken them across two countries, into places Brodie had never been, traveling by cart, afoot, then by train, forced to rely on others.

The owner of the gymnasium in London had been a much-appreciated companion in those places and cities, along

155

with Schmidt's companion, a man by the name of Vogel, who had already gone up to their room.

Schmidt had made a life for himself and his family in England, and while he'd been born in Germany and lived there half his life, he had no use for those who were bent on war. He had seen too much of that sort of thing as a young man, with endless conflict and finally oppression after the Franco-Prussian war.

"I have seen what such things do to the people," he told Brodie. "Always it is the common people who pay the price. I will help you find this person whose scheme will only kill innocent men, women, and children, to stop this if we can."

An unlikely partnership and the search had been long and bloody. The sort of thing that made friends of those who survived it.

"I need to make the crossing tonight," Brodie told the owner of the inn after receiving that telegram.

"The last ferry left hours ago," he was informed.

"What of a boat owner eager to make good money?"

The innkeeper nodded. "There is a man, if he is not out. Belvoir is his name. I can have the boy take you to him. It is not far."

"I'll go with you," Schmidt told him, "in case we have been followed."

They set off with the boy who worked at the inn, roused from sleep by the owner.

'Not far' always depended on the person who said it and what he considered 'far.'

They followed the boy to the quay south of the channel crossing, then to a fisherman's hut, the windows darkened.

The boy knocked on the door, and a woman eventually appeared. Belvoir had been gone since before daybreak and had not returned. On this sort of trip in that boat with a steam motor, they were told, he usually remained at Boulogne-Sur-Mer on the south coast, that allowed him to go out at first light for the fish.

"I am sorry, my friend," Schmidt told him as they returned to the inn. "But the lady is formidable with a weapon. I should know."

Formidable. That she was, Brodie thought.

She had gone to Munro, told him about a murder. And had then continued on her own because he wasna there.

He knew better than to leave her on her own with an inquiry case. The past two years had shown him that, and before that when he had gone to that Greek Island, sent by her ladyship.

Independent, stubborn by nature, he had never known her to give up, to walk away and abandon another. And that included himself.

Bloody hell!

There was nothing to do but wait for the first ferry that left Calais in the morning, followed by hours aboard a train from Dover.

He had taken a room, with Schmidt and Vogel in another room, but didn't go there. There was no sleep, his nerves raw, pain throbbing behind his eyes, as he sat in that darkened tavern next to the inn.

She had taught him about that—about nerves that caused pain when injured. It never had a name before, only an awareness from other encounters.

"It has been scientifically proven," she had told him when they returned to the office at the end of one of their inquiry cases and he had been struck across the back of the head.

"When a nerve is injured it sends pain to muscle. Mr. Brimley explained to me."

'Scientifically proven.'

He would have laughed at that, an explanation for something he'd discovered a long time ago on the streets.

How many other times had she spoken about something that left him shaking his head? Far different from himself and the places he had been, the things he had done.

She was educated, well-read, spoke three languages that she had shrugged off when he asked, as if it was unimportant. And she had travelled to many of those same places. A woman of the world, someone had once described her.

His experience was far different—Edinburgh and London did not count as world travel, the backstreets and alleys, the docks and the things found there.

Still, there was that way about her, when she looked at him with complete honesty that had stripped away the wall he had built around himself.

'Protection' he called it, that came from the streets, against the pain and loss, until he didna feel anything at all. Except for her.

She had torn down that wall, brick by brick, with her courage and sass, with a boldness and courage he'd never known in anyone, not even other survivors on the street. And trust that was worth its weight in gold to him.

She had spoken of it, something Lady Montgomery had told her about trust. And she had trusted him then. And now?

She was out there, somewhere, alone. And he was miles away, in another country. All because Sir Stanton had come to him with a serious proposal, information learned by the Agency about a plot against the Crown.

It was a serious threat—the people who had provided the

information had paid for it with their lives. There was someone inside the British government who had been providing highly secret information, as Avery described it. Information that included the travel schedule of diplomats, including the Foreign Secretary.

It was serious enough that he had agreed to try to find who had provided that information. And ironic, that it was Mikaela who had passed on information about a person who had recently returned from extended travel in Europe.

Sir Lionel Blandford, known to Lady Montgomery, and a passing comment that turned out to be highly important.

Stolen documents had been recovered from Sir Lionel Blandford's estate. Blandford's wife, who was German by birth, had hidden them in a false compartment in her luggage as they prepared to permanently leave the country. Both were now in cells somewhere inside the Tower.

Six bloody days ago!

Following the information Blandford had provided that included a name that he eventually revealed as he screamed with pain in that chair in the library at his estate—Novack.

Brodie left immediately for Dover, then Paris, and on to Frankfurt, Germany. To cut off the head of the snake, as Sir Avery Stanton called it.

Surely there were others better suited, Brodie had argued. But Sir Stanton had assured him that he was the perfect choice. He was unknown to any of those they were after, a stranger in those countries who could move about easily without suspicion.

He was not part of the British government or the military, with deniability if anything should go wrong. And perhaps most important, he was expendable.

He couldn't tell Mikaela any of it, couldn't tell her where he was going or when he would return.

He had accepted it. He would go, he told Stanton, but only if he could choose the people who went with him. That included Schmidt, owner of the German Gymnasium in London.

Schmidt had departed Germany twenty years earlier, but still knew people there. He also knew of Novack, the terrorist, along with the circle of persons who followed him.

There had been rumblings through the German community in London about plans to assassinate the Kaiser, overthrow the German government, and then move on to other capitols across Europe. Novack's people were loyal and the information Blandford gave them indicated they were well armed.

Schmidt accompanied Brodie to Frankfurt along with a man he trusted, from within the German community, a man called Steiger.

The underground network Novack's people had built was difficult to penetrate. Eventually there was a rumor, someone who knew someone, payment passed from hand to hand. Information learned piece by piece. It had all taken time.

Brodie understood the man's reasons for what he had planned that came from his own early experiences—the poverty and starvation, the hopelessness.

Yet innocent lives had been caught up in attacks on government buildings, a high-ranking official murdered in his bed, innocent men, women, and children killed when explosions tore through the center of cities and spared no one.

And proof in those documents found in Blandford's possession that had sent Brodie there—Novack was determined to bring down the British monarchy. A piece of information that eventually led to a man who was a foot soldier of Novack's, put in charge of procuring weapons.

They found Novack, along with several of his trusted inner circle—a great deal of money could purchase loyalty. Enough of it for the person who provided the information to disappear.

Discovered, with many of his followers choosing to flee, Novack chose not to surrender. Another man they'd met up with, who went by the name of Anatole, left Novack's body somewhere in the forest outside Frankfurt.

"Let the wolves and crows have him," Schmidt said at the time.

Afterward, on information persuaded from others, railcars full of weapons and munitions were discovered in a railyard, bound for cities across Europe.

Any one thing could easily have gone wrong. But it hadn't. The man he'd been sent to find, and a good many others, had been stopped.

"There will be a quick trial for the others," Schmidt assured him as they made their way back through the countryside in the disguise of shepherds.

"And an even quicker execution."

Brodie pinched back the pain at the bridge of his nose. His eyes burned, his body craved sleep. But there was none.

There were only the shadows in the tavern, dimly lit by a single electric light over the counter, the smell of ale and wine that mixed with that of old wood, smoke, and those who had left hours before.

And he thought of Mikaela, and the growing fear that he should have stayed in London. He should have been there to help with the case she'd taken.

Many times he had forced himself past the things she stirred in him, things he was certain were as dead as the past that he'd somehow survived. And each time, she was there with her stubbornness, a boldness that had terrified him more than once, her intelligence, and a keen understanding of things he'd never known a woman to possess. And her refusal to quit, to remain where it was safe, when everything including himself told her that she should.

When he had learned more, along with what Lady Montgomery had shared with him that first time, he recognized it.

Beneath the title, the privilege, the private education, and wealth was someone very like himself. With old wounds, the people she had loved who were gone, the strength she had pulled up from somewhere deep inside her. And that red hair that said a great deal more.

He was convinced there must be a Scot somewhere in that very long family history.

"Well," Lady Montgomery had once said. "I suppose anything is possible, Mr. Brodie. What with a few known scoundrels, along with others." she told him when he had commented on it. "I confess that I once had red hair, although you might not believe that now. I assure you that it is true."

It explained a great deal about both of them.

And now?

His fist came down on the bench where he sat against the wall of the tavern. That question that slipped through the exhaustion, and the pain that burned behind his eyes.

What if something happened to her ...?

Could he live without the stubbornness that often got her into trouble, the way she challenged and argued with him?

Could he?

The answer was there when the man who worked the tavern appeared just before first light and slammed the hinged bar top into place with a loud crack.

Then there was coffee, a great deal of it spiced with cinnamon, that she had persuaded him to add to his own preferred strong coffee. As she explained it, she had it on good authority that the spice was good for the heart.

The schedule for departures for Dover was posted inside the entrance to the tavern. There was a three-hour wait for the next boat returning to the English coast.

He downed more coffee and then finally pushed back the plate with remnants of a meal, where Schmidt and Steiger, who sat across from him, had both cleaned theirs, including most of a loaf of bread with honey and jam.

"You will do her no good if you do not eat," Schmidt told him, cutting more pieces of ham.

It wasn't food Brodie needed.

The return crossing was with the tide and far quicker than the one they'd made before. Then, the return to London by rail.

Time.

It healed all wounds, someone told him. He knew only too well that it was also an enemy.

Sir Avery Stanton would be waiting in London, anxious for word of what they'd found that he had not put in the telegram he had sent from Paris. He had sent only a brief message—Mission accomplished!

Not content to wait at the agency office at the Tower, Sir Stanton was waiting for them at the rail platform.

Brodie barely nodded in greeting and pushed past with Schmidt and Steiger.

Stanton called out over the noise on the platform of the station—conversations, excited laughter, the congestion where people boarded their train, the hiss of the steam engines.

"Brodie! I need your report!"

His report? It had been three days since anyone had seen or heard from Mikaela and that same amount of time since Munro had sent that telegram to Dover.

He stopped and shot a look back at Sir Avery Stanton.

Not that he wasn't familiar with reports from his time with the MET, and in the private inquiry business.

"The matter was taken care of, with four dead, including the one I went after, and others in custody with the authorities," he shouted across the crowd of startled passengers and others he passed as he left.

"Now," he snapped. "Ye have my report!"

Thirteen

SUSSEX SQUARE

BEFORE THE TEAM of horses came to a full stop, Brodie was already out of the coach and halfway up the steps to the main entrance.

"Munro?" he asked Mr. Symons, barely breaking stride.

"Yessir, he's here. The cellar, I believe ..."

There was more than one startled exclamation from among the servants as he made his way past the formal hall and the kitchens, then found Munro near the stairs that led to the cellar.

"I need to know," he told him. "Tell me! All of it!"

"I tried to persuade her against it, particularly when she shared what she and Mr. Dooley found at Kew," Munro explained after he had told him everything about her visit to Sussex Square.

"I went to the office afterward, but she was already gone. She must have taken herself off straightaway. She was worrit for the other women that disappeared. Ye know how she can be."

Brodie nodded. "What does Lady Antonia know of this?"

"I've not shared about Miss Mikaela's disappearance, or the

telegram that I sent ye. Given what Miss Mikaela means to her and her age, I thought it best to keep it to myself until ye returned."

"I'll tell her. She needs to know," Brodie replied. "And it's possible Mikaela might have told her something that will help us find her."

"Missing?" Lady Montgomery's exclaimed sharply, the only outward sign of any emotion as Brodie told what had happened, and what they knew.

"She said nothing of this to me," she added. "If she had ..." She paused. "That is of no consequence now, is it? What else do you know?"

He told her what Munro had learned about Mikaela's visit to Kew Mortuary, and about the inquiries she was making.

"Of course, she would not turn away from such a thing," Lady Antonia commented. "It is not in her, as you well know."

"Did she say anything when she was here?" he asked. "Anything about what she intended to do next?"

"She was only here briefly, then gone before I knew of it."

She took a deep breath.

"She is important to us both, Mr. Brodie. You will find her. Nothing else is acceptable."

"Has something happened?" Lily stood at the opening to the parlor. "Tell me," she demanded, then listened as Brodie explained what he had told Lady Antonia.

"I can help. I want to go with you."

Brodie exchanged a look with Lady Antonia. He knew the girl's attachment to Mikaela was strong. Still with one young woman dead and others missing ...

She was too much like Mikaela, and might very well take herself off to make her own inquiries. It was too dangerous, and there were too many things that were unknown. This was not for her, no matter her feelings in the matter

"Ye need to be here if she should contact her ladyship," he told her, instead of telling her 'no' outright. "That will be most helpful."

She gave him a long look that was too familiar in another. How was it, he thought, there was no blood relation between the two, yet in that moment she looked very much like Mikaela Forsythe.

"I know wot yer doin'," she replied, the Scots accent slipping around the words. "Ye think I canna help, that I'll just be in the way."

"I think she would not want ye goin' off into something that could be dangerous," Brodie told her. "And I'd not want to have to explain it to her afterward."

He didn't add his concerns about finding Mikaela, that he had no idea where she had gone, or who was behind the one girl's brutal murder.

She appeared to consider that.

"Ye will send word as soon as ye have found her?"

"Aye."

She slowly nodded. "I hold ye to that, Mr. Brodie."

"And I trust that you will bring her back safely," Lady Antonia added, much as she had told him in parting once before when she sent him off that first time.

"And you must take Mr. Munro with you. Two sets of hands are far better than one, as they say."

Brodie nodded. "I will find her."

As he turned to leave with Munro, he caught a glimpse of the two portraits of Mikaela and her sister on the wall above a side table.

According to Lady Antonia, the portraits were painted

years before, when both young women had returned from school in Paris.

Mikaela's sister was younger, with a shy smile in the one portrait, while Mikaela, with her hair down around her shoulders, had a faraway look in the expression on her face.

He had never been one to pay attention to works of art, but here the artist had captured the fire in her eyes as she stared at some distant point. Her next adventure perhaps.

He waited as Munro retrieved a weapon from his room, along with the knife that he always carried since they were lads on the street.

"We will find her," his friend assured him.

The Strand was well lit as it usually was until well into the evening, with the glow in the night sky from the nearby theater district, restaurants that remained open, pubs, and the smoke-shop next over for gentlemen who might stop by.

But the office at #204 at the top of the stairs was dark.

Mr. Cavendish was there.

Brodie shook his head. A small thing that none might have given second thought, yet among things that had changed since Mikaela Forsythe had entered his life, she had insisted on calling the man by his name.

"It is Cavendish," she had informed Brodie, something he had not known.

For him and most others on the street, the man was known as the 'Mudger,' a name the man had given when they first met a handful of years before when Brodie was still inspector with the MET.

And then there was the hound who came along later,

usually filthy with a smell that often told where he'd been—the cattle yards, the docks, and places in between.

She named him Rupert for an animal she had as a child. A side of her Brodie would not have expected.

As for himself?

That had been open to some speculation considerin' when they first met, he was in the process of retrievin' her at the request of Lady Montgomery from an island where Mikaela had taken herself off with her guide.

She had looked him in a manner that had a way of putting people in their place and said, "I think I shall not go with you."

There had been several colorful words along with that, that he thought no proper English lady would know, much less use.

She had also called him a bloody bugger and something no doubt far more colorful in French by the sound of it. Then, she had attempted to escape with the guide, and had almost succeeded.

He had made inquiries about her before leaving London.

"All of that is exaggeration," Lady Montgomery had assured him at the time. "She is her own self, of course, a bit strong-minded to be certain, but not foolish or reckless." And then that smile on the older woman's face.

"I daresay very much like myself ... But I digress."

The fee for retrieving Lady Mikaela Forsythe was substantial and he had accepted the task, yet kept in mind the rumors and Lady Antonia's explanation.

He had followed information, not unlike his other inquiry cases, across the Greek islands, to the beach where he found her scantily dressed, and then escorted her to the boat provided by her ladyship for the return trip to the port on the coast of Italy.

Along the way she had attempted to escape.

Looking back on that first meeting he realized that neither

of them had escaped. That spirit, her stubbornness, and the way she challenged him had slipped inside him, with her red hair and those eyes that were somewhere between shades of brown, then green when she had her red up.

Or it might have been when she appeared at the office quite by surprise on the recommendation of Lady Montgomery when her sister had disappeared a handful of years later.

"Lady Montgomery, my great-aunt, has said that you are someone who can be trusted, Mr. Brodie," she stated at the time, with a look that he would never forget. A challenge to be certain.

She was a lady, he told himself, although that might be somewhat in doubt by her actions.

He was not of her class. Nor was he anyone she might have otherwise encountered if not for her great-aunt's recommendation. And there was that previous, somewhat difficult situation when he had fetched her back to London.

And then there was her temper, the stubbornness, that single-mindedness, along with her insistence that she would find her sister, no matter where it took her and no matter if he was willing to help her or not.

That same stubbornness and loyalty that had taken her to Edinburgh to help him find someone, in spite of the fact that he refused to let her go with him?

It was all of it, he supposed, their partnership in his inquiry cases, friendship he had never known with a woman, that fire in her eyes when she was angry, and saints help him, he had asked her to marry him.

She had possibly surprised the both of them when she accepted.

And now? Bloody hell!

He should have been there, should have listened to her, how important the case was.

"What can ye tell me?" he asked Mr. Cavendish.

"She was stirred up about the inquiries she'd been makin' in the disappearance of me friend's daughter." He shook his head.

"There was somethin' she learned that sent her to the newspaper office and that fellow that writes for them. Burke is the man's name. I know she went there, but she didn't share what she discovered. And she kept asking for the daily afterward."

Theodolphus Burke. Not someone she cared for, in fact had called the man some colorful names in the past.

"And just three days ago, she had me take two messages to the courier's office. One was for you at the Agency, the other was to a woman by the name of Davies with an address in Marylebone. She spent hours up at the office, then left to meet the woman late that same afternoon. It was after that meetin' that she had a message from Mr. Dooley."

And as Brodie now knew, had accompanied him to Kew Mortuary when the one girl's body was found.

"The next day she kept askin' about the mornin' paper, then took herself off late in the day," Cavendish added. "I wanted her to take the hound with her and he jumped straight away into the cab." He shook his head.

"Then he comes trottin' up the Strand after she obviously sent him back, and went on alone. And now ..." He shook his head.

"I should never have asked her to try to find me friend's daughter."

Brodie laid a hand on the man's shoulder.

"The blame is not yers. As for her takin' the inquiry case on her own? That's on me."

"Where do ye want to begin?" Munro asked as Brodie turned to the stairs that led to the office.

"Find Mr. Brown. His people have an ear to everything that goes on around London. Someone may have heard something. A lady disappearin' on the streets is not a common thing," he added.

"And yerself?" Munro asked.

"I need to know if there is anything in the office that might tell me where she went that last day," he replied.

Munro nodded. "We will find her."

"Aye."

Not unexpected, when he reached it, the office door was locked.

That too was something that had changed over the past two years.

Before, he had always left the office unlocked. There was nothing of value there. But when she first stayed over, he had the lock installed.

He unlocked it now and stepped inside.

More than the lock on the door had changed. It was there in the orderliness of the place, the light that poured in through the window beside his desk, washed clean of the usual grime that he'd paid no attention to before.

It was there at her typing machine that he'd purchased for her to work on the next Emma Fortescue novel and type reports at her desk. And there was the pot that sat atop the cast-iron stove that held coffee in the morning that they shared. A cloud of chalk dust covered the wood floor beside the rubbish bin where she cleaned the felt eraser after using it on the chalkboard.

There was the furniture that had been added—her desk, a side table, and chairs for those they met with. Things that now filled the office, that anyone might not give a thought to, that filled up an empty place ... the way she had filled up empty places inside him.

And the bloody chalkboard that she insisted upon.

It was covered with notes—lists, details, questions, and things she'd learned while he was away that included the names of three young women who had disappeared, including the daughter of Mr. Cavendish's friend.

There were other names of those she'd met with—Elizabeth Davies, the mother of Charlotte Davies, and another woman at Covent Garden who knew Lizzie Smith, along with the name of a young man she'd met there.

Burke's name was there as well, more than once, as she learned some bit of information that raised another question.

But what did it mean? Had she learned something important from him?

He looked about the office, then went to her desk and searched the drawers, not that he expected to find what he sought. She always kept the notebook with her.

Did it contain more information that she hadn't an opportunity to add to the board?

Where to begin—it was like the cases he took when he was with the MET.

A missing woman, the murder of another, clues that revealed little, and time perhaps running out. Only this time, it was personal.

He placed a telephone call to the New Scotland Yard and left a message for Mr. Dooley.

～

"One of the patrols found the girl's body," Dooley explained after receiving the message Brodie had sent him. He shook his head.

"In all my time with the MET, I've never seen such a thing. Not even with those poor women over in Whitechapel."

Brodie had worked with Dooley when he was with the MET, and many times since. He was a good man and he trusted him.

"Did she say anything when ye left the mortuary?"

"She only asked who would do such a thing? Then she thanked me and said not another word about what she saw at Kew. Not even when we went to the Bond Street Station for her to make a statement about what she knew about the poor girl.

"I escorted her to Mayfair afterward. Now, tell me. What has happened?"

"She has disappeared. It seems that she might have gone somewhere as part of her inquiries, and she's not been back in almost three days."

Mr. Dooley's expression was grim. He nodded. "How can I help?"

"Follow any lead ye might have, and let me know what you find. If I'm not here, leave word with Mr. Cavendish."

Mr. Dooley nodded. "We have the information on the other two young women that disappeared. I'll put the word out with the lads. And contact me as well if you learn something important."

When he left, Brodie went back to the chalkboard.

The last entry she had made was on 18 June. It obviously meant something important, and according to what Mr. Cavendish had told him, that was the last time he saw her when she had him call for a cab, and had then sent the hound back.

Three days ago.

How was it all connected?

He read through everything on the board again and came back to an entry for The Times newspaper with a question mark added with each entry.

What had she learned when she went see Mr. Burke at The Times?

There was nothing to indicate what it might have been. Perhaps nothing. Or possibly something she hadn't taken the time to add to the board ...

Then that entry that seemed to verify what Mr. Cavendish had told him, that she had asked to see the latest edition of the newspaper, and had then taken herself off the afternoon of 18 June.

What was in the newspaper that had sent her off hours later?

It was late in the day when he left the office, the Strand crowded with end-of-day traffic and congestion, as a driver finally arrived and Brodie gave him the location of the newspaper office on Fleet Street.

The ground floor office and attendant's desk were still well lit when he arrived, in spite of the late hour.

"Mr. Burke," he told the young clerk at the desk.

"He left some time ago, sir. Is there something I can help with?"

"Where would he go?" Brodie demanded.

"I don't know exactly ..." the young man stammered.

"Perhaps some place when he leaves early of the day?" Brodie replied, rapidly losing patience.

"Possibly the Punch Tavern. He goes there sometimes to meet others who work at the other papers ..."

The Punch Tavern was on the corner of Fleet Street, a

typical London pub, filled with workers at the end of the day, and Theodolphus Burke.

They'd had previous encounters when Brodie was at the MET and then on a well-known inquiry case that involved the royal family. His opinion of the man was much the same as Mikaela's.

There was a round of laughter where Burke stood at the long bar, a gin glass in his hand. By the laughter, it obviously was not his first of the night as he told his companions a story.

"Mr. Burke, a word," Brodie told him, as he joined the man at the bar.

Burke turned with a frown, his story interrupted, and looked at him with a narrowed gaze. Recognition made its way through the gin haze.

"Are the police about to raid the place?" he asked with a smirk. "Should we all flee for our lives? Oh, yes, I have forgotten. You are no longer part of that distinguished brotherhood.

"I remember now," he continued. "You now make private inquiries and with a woman, I might add, Lady 'something or other.' Though hardly a lady the way she goes about the city."

It was the drink, Brodie told himself. He'd seen it a thousand times on the street and for now, chose to ignore the insult.

"You met with her just days ago. I need to know the reason. It's important."

"A man who cannot keep his position with the MET, and now cannot keep a woman in her place?" Burke raised his gin glass as if making a toast. "I will admit, aggravating as the woman is, she is a handsome piece."

The glass sailed out of his hand as Brodie seized him by the collar of his coat, picked him up off the floor, and slammed him against the bar.

The tavern had suddenly gone quiet.

"We have business, Mr. Burke. We can discuss it here, or back at your office," Brodie told him. "But you will tell me wot I want to know."

There was a quick nod in response.

"I thought so." He dragged Theodolphus Burke from the tavern, and then 'escorted' him back to The Times newspaper building.

"What information was she after?" Brodie asked a slightly bruised Burke who sat uneasily on the chair at his desk as if he was uncertain what might happen next.

"What information was she looking for?" Brodie repeated. "I'll not ask it again."

Except for their somewhat one-sided conversation, the office was quiet save for a night clerk on the ground floor and a young reporter who had been working after the usual business hours and had decided that could be done elsewhere.

"It was regarding an advertisement that ran in the paper," Burke replied somewhat shakily. "Something she found and wanted to know who had put it in the paper."

"Tell me, all of it, or I will stay here until you do."

There was no need to threaten the man further.

It was an advertisement on the front page of the newspaper —on the Personals Page for companionship of various natures —matrimony, affairs, the connection to a woman who offered her services, and companionship.

The advertisement Mikaela wanted information on was regarding the last one—'companionship for travel,' that she had apparently come by with the inquiries that she was making.

"I explained to her that I did not have any knowledge of the advertisements for the Personals Page."

"Who has the information?" Brodie snapped.

"Mr. Charles on the third floor."

"Did she go to the third floor to see the man?"

Burke nodded.

"And where is this man now?"

"He works quite late preparing the ads for the morning edition. He may still be there."

Brodie hauled him out of the chair. "Then we will pay a visit to the third floor."

Howard Charles was there, bent over a large sheet of paper, making marks as he scanned it, thick glasses on his face.

He looked up at the intrusion, startled at the sight of Theodolphus Burke being dragged along like a reluctant hound.

"What the devil ...?" he exclaimed.

"I have need of information," Brodie told the poor man whose hair—what there was of it—stood up about his head and gave the appearance of one of those 'fright' drawings the paper printed from time to time to stir up their customers.

He explained about the series of advertisements identified by that box number 41984, the first placed months before. Over that time there had been responses.

"Everything is confidential, as I told the lady," Mr. Charles added after Brodie explained the information he was after.

The responses to that box number were then picked up weekly by a representative or servant of the person who placed the advertisement.

Also part of that confidentiality, no names were ever exchanged due to the nature of some of the ads.

"I want to know about the advertisement that ran the last several weeks and the responses that were received and then passed on to the owner of the ad."

"As I explained ..."

Again there was that hesitance, on behalf of confidentiality. Brodie took out the revolver and pressed it against Burke's head.

"And I thank ye kindly," he told both men when he finally had the tear-sheets from those past issues that, at a glance, told him what Mikaela might have been after.

He paused briefly at the door to that third-floor department.

"Mr. Burke," he directed what he said next to the reporter. "You are apparently somewhat educated. So you will understand what I say and my meanin'. She is very much a lady, and if I ever learn that you have insulted her in any way, I will see that you never speak again. Make of that what you will."

Outside The Times offices, he found a driver and returned to the office on the Strand.

The original advertisement that had been the same each time was not unusual. It was unusual in that Mikaela had taken it with her for her meeting with Burke:

Seeking female companion for same, for travel and adventure.
Age 18-25. All expenses paid.
No whores or prostitutes need reply.
Respond #41984.

And the response she'd made just after that visit to the that same box number:

#41984
I am a respectable girl of the age required.
I am a hard worker and wish to travel.
Awaiting your reply.

Brodie knew how she thought and the language of the response was articulate—'Awaiting your reply.'

They were not the words of a flower seller at Covent Garden or a young woman who worked in her father's shop.

It made sense that she had placed an answer to that ad. It's what he would have done in order to find the person responsible for them. And she had received a response:

'Respectable Girl. We must meet.
3:00
18 Jun.
#4 Princes Gate, Knightsbridge'

He had an address and was certain that was where she had gone.

Fourteen

MIKAELA

HOW MUCH TIME HAD PASSED? A day? Longer?

It was difficult to know, as I was now locked in a different room with no clock after I had discovered Simon La Geness's very own private gallery.

With that sword at my back, he had walked me to another part of the manor on that floor, through a hallway darkened except for the lantern he held, and then forced me into this room. Then, to make certain that I did not escape again, he had bound my wrists and tied me to a chair.

"You cannot hide what you've done," I told him. "The others you brought here…"

"I have done nothing wrong," he insisted, suddenly quite emotional. "It's nothing more than young women responding to the advertisement for travel."

How was it possible that he so easily excused what he'd done? The young women who had disappeared? Lizzie Smith murdered?

Had she refused to pose for him once she learned the purpose of those ads? And now?

I could only assume that he had no intention they would ever be released, or his scheme would be exposed. As for myself ...

That seemed obvious as well.

He was mad, it was the only explanation.

"Once the paintings are seen, people will know what you've done ..." I told him. "There will be no hiding it."

"I will take the collection to Paris, where little attention will be given to who the models were, but instead, to the work itself. You saw how the people of London responded at the gallery."

"You have to know that I was asked to make inquiries on behalf of one of the women," I informed him, without providing a name. "Others will become suspicious. Especially ..."

"When a lady of society disappears?" he suggested. He brushed a lock of hair that had spilled over his forehead. His hand trembled noticeably as it had the night of the reception at the Grosvenor.

"As I have said, your arrival here was ... unexpected and most unfortunate," he continued, dropping his hand to his side as if to hide it. "Yet, I will not deny that I very much wanted to paint a portrait of you after meeting you at the gallery.

"I thought, of course, that your portrait would have to be made from memory. Not that I haven't done that before."

Of course, I thought, a face glimpsed in the crowd, as he had explained it, then remembered and used for his next subject.

"The gown you were wearing that night," he continued. "A

color very much like dark wine, and as you have seen, very much the same in the painting."

I had seen madness before, but this …

"And after you have finished the portrait? The same fate as Lizzie Smith?"

He seemed surprised. "A foolish girl, but a lady of society, known for her penchant for travel." He shrugged. "It will be considered nothing more than you have simply taken yourself off again on another adventure.

"As for your likeness in the portrait? It will be easily explained as I have already said—an encounter at the gallery and the desire to capture your likeness if anyone should question it."

I sadly thought of Gwen Tavers and Charlotte Davies and the fate that no doubt awaited them as well.

"Ah, yes," he said then. "That is the expression that is needed for your portrait—just a touch of sadness, you are perhaps wistful. Far different from the others and fascinating, in my attempt to capture what your thoughts must be."

I thought of those other portraits in the exhibit at the Grosvenor Gallery. Other young women drawn into his mad scheme?

The possibility was horrifying.

"You will remain here, for now," he said as he turned to leave. "It is more comfortable here than in the rooms below."

As if I was a guest he was entertaining.

"You cannot escape," he said. "The door will be locked, and watched at all times."

By a loyal servant? Perhaps the same one who had attacked me earlier? Possibly the same person who had killed Lizzie Smith?

He frowned. "There must be time to finish the portrait.

You must not struggle to free yourself—the rope can bruise flesh terribly. You could scream, but as I am certain you have already discovered, there is no one to hear you. And I could not bear to see your lovely face marred."

He turned to leave, but not before reaching out. I drew back as far as possible at the touch of his fingers as he angled my face toward the light from an oil lamp.

Was there regret perhaps in the way his fingers trembled? He cursed and made a fist of his hand clenched in the other.

"*Oui*, of course. It is just that look in your eyes," he added.

I heard the door lock from the outside as the metal lever clicked into place when he left, and then his footsteps gradually faded.

I slowly let out the breath I had taken at the touch of his fingers and fought to collect my thoughts.

I had to find a way out of that room and then find Gwen Tavers, Charlotte Davies, and any others whose faces I had seen on those portraits.

He had left the oil lamp behind. To prevent my being frightened in a darkened room? How very considerate.

Yet what La Geness had in store was far more frightening than a darkened room.

I glanced about for some means to rid myself of the rope that bound me to the chair.

The room had obviously been used as a dressing room, with a screen, table, and another chair, a full-length mirror, undoubtedly where the next young woman was prepared for her portrait sitting.

Without knowing either Gwen Tavers or Charlotte Davies, I tried to imagine what they must have felt when they were each brought to this room—confusion, fear, then helplessness?

It was not difficult to imagine as their hopes and excitement for the opportunity of travel were dashed by the reality of what they had found here. Had either of them fought back and attempted to escape?

It was possible that Gwen Tavers might have. I did not have the impression that she was either shy or weak. As for Charlotte Davies ... I did not know.

Her family was well placed, she'd been given a proper education. I knew only what I had seen in her sister—strength, certainly.

She would have needed that for what awaited the women here, along with their dashed hopes for adventure in far places.

I glanced over at the side table. A ceramic pitcher and glass had been left there. For water that I couldn't pour? I almost laughed.

So very kind of Monsieur La Geness, I thought, with no small amount of sarcasm that was far better than giving in to the fear of what waited if I was not able to free myself.

I looked at the pitcher again. Once broken, a piece of it might be used to cut the rope.

Neither my legs or ankles were bound. Difficult as it was, tied to that chair, I pushed to my feet, then slowly made my way across the room, dragging it with me.

It was exhausting, as I stopped, then began again, much like an enormous turtle I had once seen. It was awkward, clumsy, and I was certain that I might crash to the floor at any moment.

I eventually reached the table, then eased my shoulder under the edge and attempted to rock it back and forth in an effort to topple that pitcher.

It took more than one effort, but eventually the pitcher toppled to the floor and broke into several pieces. One of those pieces was the pitcher handle.

If I could reach it, I might be able to use it to cut the rope.

I thought of that turtle again as I rocked the chair from side to side, and finally managed to send it over and landed hard on the floor.

I lay there for several moments, expecting someone to charge through the door at any moment. When that didn't happen, I managed to move closer to those shattered pieces of the pitcher until I was able to grab that broken handle.

As I lay there, trussed up like a Christmas goose for market, I began to slice at the rope. A sound at the door stopped me. It suddenly opened.

I fully expected La Geness or perhaps the person who had attacked me earlier, having heard the sound of my fall. Instead, I stared into large brown eyes in the thin face of a young girl.

"*Non! Non!*" she frantically whispered as she glanced back over her shoulder, then back at me. And still in French, "*This cannot be!*"

I was not certain who was more surprised as we stared at each other. It appeared that my 'guard' was in fact a child of no more than perhaps nine or ten years, and terrified.

She glanced over her shoulder once more, then quickly came into the room and closed the door behind her.

"*Non, non!*" she repeated as she knelt beside me, clearly upset. "*Il y a du sang!*"

Blood?

I glanced down at my hands.

I saw only a slight cut on one hand, certainly nothing to be upset about under the circumstances. Yet she was extremely distraught to the point of tears.

"*Blood, where?*" I asked in French.

Obviously surprised that I not only understood what she

said but spoke French as well, she patted her fingers against her own cheek, and repeated the word for blood.

It appeared that I had managed to cut myself when I sent the chair over and landed on the floor amid the shattered pieces of the pitcher.

I was hardly in a position to be upset over a little blood. But that might certainly create a problem for La Geness's plans for that portrait. I felt no sympathy there.

The situation was not at all what I might have expected. How was it that a child was even there, much less left to guard that door?

Before I could say more, she took the hem of her gown and gently pressed it against my cheek.

"What is your name?" I asked in French.

It was *Jolie*, she replied, terrified that it would be discovered that I had attempted to escape.

I then asked if she could untie my wrists so that I could see how bad the cut was?

She refused at first, and backed away with another glance toward the door. She obviously expected someone to come through it at any moment, as did I.

What was she doing there? Was she La Geness's daughter?

That hardly seemed to be the case. She was unbelievably thin, barefoot, and her gown was badly faded and stained. And there was the fear I saw on her face.

Was it possible that she was held against her will? Like others who had been brought here?

"You are the English lady I heard them speak of?" she asked.

I nodded.

She had unknowingly answered one of my questions. La Geness had not acted in this alone.

I then asked in French. "Were there other women brought here like myself?"

She nodded, then looked to the door once more.

They would beat her if they found out that she was talking to me, she whispered. And then she would end up like the others.

I explained that I had come to help them ... and I could help her. But first, I needed her help, I needed her to untie the rope.

I saw the fear and desperation in the expression at her face, and for a moment I was certain she would refuse.

Then her expression changed, and I saw something of what I had seen in Lily when we first met in Edinburgh, the strength hidden there. Along with hope.

"I will help you," she said then. "But you must promise to take me with you."

I assured her that I would. She then knelt behind me on the floor, and I felt her tug at the rope. It went slack. I pulled it away, freeing myself from the chair, then slowly pushed to my feet.

We stood there, looking at each other, perhaps both trying to figure out what the other would do next. She did not shout for help, and even now stood only a few feet away with that hesitant expression on her face.

I complimented her for being very brave and asked how old she was. And like Lily, she did not know.

I then asked how she came to be there.

"They bought me on the street in Paris."

The words tore at me. However, I was not surprised. I knew that it happened far too often on the streets of London, and obviously in other places as well.

"Will you leave me here now that you are free of the rope?" she asked.

"I don't break my promises," I replied. "We will leave together."

My heart ached for her—so very young, no doubt abandoned, and then left to a fate with someone like La Geness.

She had spoken of '*them*' again. I needed to know who else was part of this mad scheme, and asked who they were.

"Monsieur and the woman," she replied. "And there is a man who works for them. I do not like him."

She then asked if I was the woman in the painting.

I explained that I was not that woman, that it was an illusion of La Geness's imagination.

"No," I replied. "I am not, but he wants me to be."

And then a horrifying thought. Was he perhaps grooming her to be a model for one of his portraits? To then be gotten rid of like the others?

"There are others. Do you know where they are?" I asked.

She slowly nodded.

Fifteen

BRODIE

"WHAT OF INSPECTOR Dooley and the MET?" Munro asked. "Do we wait?"

Brodie shook his head. He knew how the MET worked—permission needed for additional constables in an area that wasn't patrolled often, then questions from those high up, more hours spent explainin' what he'd learned from the man at The Times. And more time wasted as he explained the possible connection to the girl who had been murdered.

And the matter very likely set aside with the MET once more under the command of Chief Inspector Abberline—'not a priority when there were other crimes to be investigated.'

He told Munro what he'd learned from Burke and Mr. Charles at the newspaper, the questions Mikaela had asked, and the information that the advertising manager had provided in those tear-sheets.

Munro nodded. "Knightsbridge. I've not been invited

there in some time," he commented, with more than a little sarcasm.

"It's the place where that upper-class department store burnt, some time ago?"

"Aye." Brodie nodded.

Harrod's had burned to the ground a handful of years earlier. But other upper-class shops, restaurants, and businesses had continued to fill the district. He drew a crude map on the chalkboard.

"Princes Gate is where the women who responded to that ad were told to meet, in the old part of Knightsbridge. Many of the country manors there have been abandoned or taken down.

"What's there has been taken over by tenant farmers, making a living the best they can for now," he continued to explain. "Along with homeless people with nowhere to go and thieves, until all the old properties are gone." He drew a line at the north end of the district.

"Princes Gate, runs along the edge of the old part of Knightsbridge next to an old river bed. Number 4 would be here." He marked an X on the board.

"What do we know about the people we might find there?" Munro asked.

"At least three other women answered that advertisement. One has been found murdered. I dinna know how many more may have responded, or who is behind it. It's safe to say the women may be guarded. As for others ..."

Unknown.

"We'll find out when we get there," Munro replied.

"Take the hound," Mr. Cavendish told him as they waited for a driver. "He'll find her."

Brodie knew that the hound had a particular liking for Mikaela and he'd proven to be a good tracker. Yet she had chosen not to take him with her.

She had answered that advertisement as if she was simply another young woman eager for adventure. If she had shown up to that appointment with the hound, it would have caused suspicion.

What had she found when she got there? What of the other young women? Was it nothing more than a scheme to lure them? For what purpose?

He knew the usual answer to that—prostitution, and he swore.

He also knew what her reaction would have been to that, to finding others that had been lured into it. She would fight back, and with the usual persons who ran those schemes, it would cost her, dearly.

He should have been there, should have been with her! Now he had to find her.

He glanced down at the beast on the sidewalk that waited expectantly, one ear cocked forward, the other flopped over— an injury from an encounter on the street.

There was no mistaking the hound might be able to find her even before they did ... if she was still alive.

"Aye, get on with ye, then," he told the bloody animal.

He could have sworn the beast grinned.

MIKAELA

Even with the darkened hallways, Jolie knew every step, each turn in the hallway leading to a door at the other end of the floor that concealed the servant's passage.

I could only imagine how she had discovered it—perhaps desperate to hide from La Geness, stumbling upon it. Possibly hiding there?

After we left that room, I listened for the sound that anyone had discovered the empty room and followed us. For now, it seemed that no one was aware that I had escaped.

"The steps are dangerous," Jolie whispered as she opened the door and disappeared into that looming darkness.

I discovered exactly what she meant as I took the first step and felt it give slightly. Time had deteriorated the wood steps, and I could smell rot from the damp wall. I tested each one as I followed her, keeping to the side where the steps seemed to be stronger.

"We must leave ..." Jolie said in a low voice just ahead of me.

Leave?

What about the other women who were here? I had come for them and would not leave without them.

I started to protest as I came up behind her and realized that we'd reached another door along the passage. I felt a hand clasp my arm in silent warning.

We waited, hardly daring to breathe, as I heard La Geness just beyond the door, and the instructions he gave someone.

"The same as the others. There must be no trouble ... we leave soon."

There was a brief comment in response, followed by the sound of footsteps that gradually faded.

"Quickly!" Jolie tugged on my hand and we continued past that door and farther down that narrow passage.

We eventually reached the end of the stairway and another door.

It opened onto the main floor very near what had obviously once been the servants' quarters, glimpsed in the faint light shown from that room. And also the kitchen, according to what my companion whispered.

Someone—possibly a servant, abruptly left the kitchen and slowly approached with lantern in hand where we hid in that stairway.

Through that narrow slit in the door, I glimpsed a woman.

It was only a fleeting glimpse and admittedly the light was poor as she continued past with only the light from the lantern she carried. Yet for a moment, there was something familiar.

"*La madame,*" Jolie whispered, and when the woman was gone, she stepped out into the hallway.

La Geness's wife?

A memory stirred, a question my sister had asked the night of the reception at the Grosvenor. And La Geness had replied that his wife had remained in Paris.

A servant perhaps, as I first assumed. Yet Jolie had called her *La Madame*.

There was no time to question her about it, nor would I risk being heard as I quickly followed her through the shadows to the kitchen where the woman had been. Jolie moved with the confidence of someone who had done this before.

I could barely make out the shape of a long table, the large hearth behind it, and remnants of kitchen utensils that hung on a wall.

I grabbed a cleaver as Jolie reached for something that hung beside those utensils—a key.

She was cautious as we returned to the hall, then past eerie shapes of stuffed animals and sculptures that loomed up out of the shadows, lit by the ghostly light of the moon that spilled through the windows of a once elegant drawing room.

At the far end of the drawing room, Jolie pulled open a door that creaked in the silence of the large room.

We quickly left and entered what had once been a garden, now overgrown from neglect.

Once we were beyond the manor, I asked once more about the others. She replied for me to follow her.

It was nightfall once more, the sun low at the horizon, and a full day past when I first arrived, as I followed her through overhanging branches of trees. And then onto a well-worn path in the pale moonlight.

I smelled the change in the air from that verdant overgrown scent of grass and trees to the smell of stagnant water as a large stone building loomed up out of the shadows.

It was a water gate with an enormous water wheel that stood motionless but had undoubtedly once provided water to the manor from the nearby stream that gleamed in the moonlight.

The gatehouse was built of thick cut stone with a slate roof. A door at the side of the building was made of stout wood with an iron latch, secured by a large iron padlock.

It was obvious that Jolie had been here before as she inserted the key she had retrieved and unlocked the padlock.

The smell of stagnant water was strong here as we stepped inside, the bottom of my boots sucked into mud on the floor, no doubt from water that seeped in from the nearby stream.

I followed her as she crossed the large wheelhouse to an adjacent chamber, filled with the shadows of barrels and other shapes along the near wall in the light that spilled down from that roof overhead, where tiles had broken and fallen through.

One of the shadows moved, and Jolie called out in halting English, "You are safe."

I stared through the shadows as a slender figure slowly emerged from the shadows along that wall, followed by another, and then another.

I'd had only that single photograph from her father to know what she looked like, and the young woman I saw now was quite thin, her hair tangled about her shoulders with bruises at her face.

Yet, I was certain I had just found Gwen Tavers.

She had obviously been beaten. Her gown—what remained of it—was torn and hung on her like a shroud.

Horrifying as it was, I immediately thought of the portraits displayed at the Grosvenor, and I could only imagine who those other young women might have been.

My heart ached at what I saw, then came the anger that only sharpened as the others emerged from the shadows—one who appeared younger than Gwen, and then Charlotte Davies, the resemblance to her sister unmistakable.

"Who are you?" Gwen whispered haltingly, her mouth badly swollen.

"Your father asked me to find you," I replied as the others slowly gathered about me.

"How did you find us?" Charlotte asked.

I gestured to Jolie, who stood silently near the entrance to that chamber. "She showed me where you were."

The rest of it, deciphering that advertisement that I'd discovered in Gwen's room, then my conversation with Howard Charles, would all have to wait. There wasn't time now.

"Our angel," Charlotte whispered. "She brought food for us, but was always guarded."

An angel indeed, I thought.

"We tried to leave ..." Gwen explained. "But we were caught." She put her arm around the younger woman's shoulders.

"You can see what they did," Charlotte added, her voice breaking softly.

Both were bruised and there was dried blood on the mouth of the other girl, who was introduced as Molly. I recognized her from one of the portraits at La Geness's hidden gallery.

I looked around that small chamber. "Are there others?"

Gwen nodded, and pressed her fingers against her swollen mouth. "A young woman by the name of Lizzie, but she hasn't returned after that last time she was sent for. And the man came for another girl, Sarah, this morning."

There was no need to tell them about Lizzie's murder now. There would be time enough for that once they were all far from there and safe.

"Where was she taken?" I asked.

"To the manor," Gwen replied, her voice stronger now, along with the anger that came with it.

"It's what they do! They send him, and we're taken upstairs in that horrible place. He forces us to drink wine, it's horrible and bitter. Then we're forced to sit for hours ..."

Was the wine drugged? And then they were forced to sit for those portraits. It did not surprise me.

A drug in the wine to make them cooperate and for that particular expression that La Geness was after?

What sort of person would do such a thing?

Yet I knew. I had heard it in that conversation with La Geness, and he obviously intended the same for me. But it was not myself I was frightened for now.

Another young woman, Sarah, had been taken out of their

prison. I could only hope that it was not for the same reason that Lizzie Smith had disappeared.

"How many are there besides the artist and his wife?" I asked.

Were there more?

"There is a man with them," Charlotte replied. "He brought us here, but didn't speak. He is frightening, and dangerous."

"And there is a stableman," Gwen added. "We heard the sound of horses, and orders he was given ... after they took Lizzie away. That was when we tried to escape."

That was at least four people including the woman, perhaps more Gwen and the others were not aware of. And Jolie.

"But that door is aways locked," Gwen continued. "And whenever they came for one of us, they threatened the others if we tried to escape again."

It had become a prison and those inside threatened— forced to sit for long hours for those haunting portraits I had seen in that gallery on the third floor, and then ...

It was too horrible to think of what would happen next to them, as I thought of Lizzie Smith, a memory that would haunt me for a very long time.

Now, to find a way to get them out of there without being seen. If I could get them to the high road, it was possible they might be able to find a coach.

"Can you walk?" I looked first at Gwen then Charlotte.

They all nodded.

"The high road is not far from the street, then into the new part of Knightsbridge." I looked at Gwen who seemed stronger than the others.

"I know it," she nodded.

Everything I'd brought with me of any use or value was in my travel bag, which was taken when I was attacked in that first-floor room.

"You will need to find a coach."

I looked down, the plain bronze band cool on my finger. I gave her the only thing of value I still had ... my wedding ring.

"This should pay the fare to the nearest police station. Ask for Inspector Dooley. And you must take Jolie with you."

"What do we tell the police?" Charlotte asked. "What is your name?"

"Tell him all of it, he'll know."

"What are you going to do?" Gwen asked.

"I'm going to find Sarah."

Her hand closed around my wrist. "I'll go with you."

Even after everything she'd obviously been through. I shook my head.

"Go with the others," I told her. "They will need you to help them find the High Street."

"You don't know what Sarah looks like."

It wouldn't be difficult to find her, I thought, thinking of those portraits and the gallery where they had all been taken one by one.

"She has a sweet smile," Gwen said then.

As they prepared to leave, I explained to Jolie that she was to go with them.

She refused at first, but I assured her that I would join them, along with Sarah. She slowly nodded, then threw her arms around my neck.

"*Merci.*"

Thank you, I thought. Brave girl.

I handed Gwen the meat cleaver I'd taken from the kitchen at the manor.

"If anyone tries to stop you ..."

She nodded, a determined expression amid the bruises on her face.

"I know how to use it."

"Go now," I told her. "Keep to the tree-line. It's the long way around to the street beyond, but it will make it difficult for anyone to see you."

I followed them to the door of the wheel house, then waited until they had made it into the cover of the trees as they made their way toward Princes Gate Street and the High Street beyond.

I watched for any sign of movement from the manor, any indication that anyone had seen the women leave, then quickly crossed that overgrown green and returned through those double doors where Jolie and I had escaped.

BRODIE

THE DRIVER LEFT the brightly lit streets of the newer part of Knightsbridge with its upmarket shops and restaurants behind, and continued into the old part of the district, where a handful of abandoned manors still stood.

It was lit only by an occasional gas lamp, then not at all as they reached Princes Gate, the shadows of two abandoned manor houses looming up out of the moonlight.

Once grand country homes Brodie heard had been there for over two hundred years. Now waiting to make way for rowhouses, newer residences, and other shops as the railroad pushed through to this part of the city.

"Wait," Brodie told the driver, a man who regularly worked the Strand, and had provided transportation in the past.

Then he and Munro set off afoot toward Number 4 Princes Gate.

The bloody place was enormous, one of the grand manors

of old land owners who'd left long ago—three floors with countless rooms where anyone might hide, all darkened beyond that sagging wrought-iron gate and the forest of trees that had gradually taken over.

"Too many places where she might be," Munro said in a low voice. "How do you want to do this?"

In the past, as lads on the streets, they would have both carefully approached the place, let themselves inside to grab whatever might be of value, and then leave just as quickly.

But this was not the streets of Edinburgh, and what he was after was far too valuable to risk having Mikaela harmed or worse if they should encounter more than a handful of those inside. It was best to split up, and gain as much advantage as possible by entering from separate directions.

"Circle round and take the hound with ye. Take care and find a way inside. I'll go in the main entrance."

He caught Munro's nod in the pale moonlight, his expression one he'd seen a hundred times and more. Along with that smile that flashed a deadly expression.

"Aye, and meet in the middle."

They continued past that sagging gate, then Munro whistled softly and disappeared with the hound toward the far end of the manor as Brodie pushed his way through the overgrowth and hanging tree limbs then up the steps to the main entrance.

The main door was locked. The lock was one of the older ones he'd often encountered, and there was no light to see even if he could have picked it. He moved to the adjacent windows that framed the entrance.

The glass on the windows was thin, and several already broken, as others had no doubt discovered in an attempt to enter. He enlarged the opening of one beside the door with his elbow, the sound of broken glass on the flagstones of the landing.

When there was no response to that sound, he reached inside, felt the cool iron of the lever, then found the bolt, and turned it.

The door slowly swung open. Again he waited for any sign that someone had heard it. When no one appeared, he retrieved the revolver from the waist of his trousers and stepped inside.

The head of a bear looked down on him from the wall with a once elegant carved side table and a marble bust, as he slowly made his way down the hallway past what had once been a formal parlor, then to an adjacent room. He nudged the door open with the toe of his boot.

Light from the moon spilled through windows into what appeared to be a sitting room for the lord of the manor. Through the shadows he glimpsed the humped shape of an overstuffed chaise and settee across from it, his footsteps muted by the carpet.

He slowly moved around the room to better see what was there that might tell him something.

His boot brushed something soft. He started to walk around it, then realized that it was Mikaela's travel bag.

He opened it and swore as he knelt in the shadows. It still contained her revolver, notebook, and the knife Munro had made certain she always carried. She would not have left it there unless she was forced to.

When? And where was she now?

Finding nothing else that might provide the answers, he pocketed the knife and revolver, then returned to the hallway.

A shadow loomed up out of the other shadows, a man by the size of him, short and stout with an overgrown beard and a bulk that told him the man was strong. He wore a coat that hung to the knees and a wary expression that immediately turned to a snarl. The blade of the knife the man drew gleamed in the half-light in the hallway.

~

MIKAELA

As I entered the drawing room I heard a sound, faint at first, then stronger as I reached the hallway where Jolie and I had fled. It came from one of the upper floors. It appeared that my escape from that room was discovered.

I glanced toward the servant's area and kitchen, but saw no one, then heard it again, clearer followed by a terrified scream, then sound of weeping that was suddenly silenced. Sarah?

I ran up the stairs, stumbled in the dark, then pushed back to my feet as I heard that terrified scream once again. I reached the second-floor landing, and realized that it came from the third floor. I ran to the next set of stairs and followed the sound of weeping, along with a woman's voice.

"What did you see? The woman who was in this room! Tell me!"

Then the sound of more weeping, hysterical now, then begging.

I rushed toward the room where I had been bound only a short while earlier, and found a young woman cowering at another blow, and knew that I had found Sarah, as the woman I had seen in the kitchen stood over her with the blunt end of a horse whip, her arm raised to strike again.

Surprise came first, followed by confusion as I recognized her. It was the same woman I had seen at the gallery that night staring back at me. It was only a glimpse that night, but I was certain it was the same woman.

"I will not let you or anyone else ruin my work!" she screamed at the young woman, who wore only a thin wrap around her trembling shoulders with angry red welts on her back.

"Tell me where she is!" the woman screamed at her.

Her work? Her paintings?

She raised her arm to strike again.

My revolver and the knife were gone, obviously taken when I was attacked in that room below. But I would not let her continued. Angry, afraid for the girl, I ordered the woman to stop in French so there was no misunderstanding.

"You will not hurt her again!"

Sarah whimpered as the woman spun around.

"You!" she hissed at me. "How did you get out of here?" And then, "Jolie! Where is she?"

"She is with the others. They are safe now," I replied. "Unlike Lizzie Smith."

Her eyes narrowed as Sarah let out a startled, wounded sound.

"You told us that she went home," she whispered.

"Worthless girl! She would have ruined everything. I had to be rid of her. And you ...!" she spat at me.

"He insisted that he had to have a painting of you! Difficult, but not impossible after I saw you that night. Do you understand? They are *my* paintings, *my* work after he could no longer hold a brush. But they would never recognize the paintings by a *woman*!"

"You killed her?" Sarah whispered through bruised lips. Then, screamed at the woman.

"You killed her!"

The woman turned on Sarah, her arm raised to strike her.

That scream brought his head up, eyes narrowed, as Brodie lowered the body of the man who'd attacked him to the floor.

And then another scream …

He found the stairs and ran to the landing at the second floor, then ran down the long hall to the opposite end when he heard another scream, and took the stairway that led up to the third floor.

He was cautious if there should be other men like the one he'd left below, then stepped onto the landing and slowly entered a long room that appeared to be some sort of private gallery.

In the light from a lantern on a table, he saw a half dozen paintings on artist easels along the far wall.

All of the paintings were of barely dressed young women, two no more than girls, and one naked as she reclined on the settee—that same settee that sat across from the display. Two other paintings were unfinished. He stared at a third unfinished portrait.

The woman in the painting was turned away from the artist, her face in profile, her shoulders and back naked where the dark red gown she wore gaped away and exposed the length of her back.

It was unfinished, yet the woman was beautiful, her expression defiant, like that of a proper lady who had been caught as she undressed, her dark red hair falling over a bare shoulder, and the angle of her chin as she stared back from the canvas.

It was a look he knew well, the same look of a slightly younger woman with that same defiant spirit in that portrait at Sussex Square.

"Putain!"

Whore! A word Brodie knew from the streets, followed by another scream, different this time, like that of a wounded animal.

He ran toward that sound.

<h1 style="text-align:center">Seventeen</h1>

MIKAELA

I STOOD over Madame La Geness—or whoever she was. She had landed hard on the floor after I swept her feet from under her.

She screamed then cursed as she lost the whip and fought to retrieve it. I brought the heel of my boot down hard on her wrist and outstretched hand.

She screamed again, her wrist trapped under my bootheel.

"*Arrêt*!" I told her in French. "Stop! Or I promise you that I will crush your hand, and you will never feed yourself again, much less paint another portrait!"

I was calm, deliberate as I bent over her, the lessons I'd learned years before of that ancient discipline there as I told her.

"Or possibly your neck for what you have done!"

She stared up at me through pain and growing fear that I might do exactly as I threatened.

In that moment, I was equally certain that I would do

exactly that, and with little remorse as I thought of Lizzie Smith and the other young women I'd found in that gatehouse.

And for those few moments, her uncertainty and my determination hung in the air between us.

"Miss?" Sarah whispered, drawing my attention.

I looked over at her and saw the change in the expression on her face go from fear to confusion as she stared past me.

And then felt a hand on my shoulder.

"Mikaela?"

A voice I knew. Impossible ... I turned.

Brodie?

"Miss!" Sarah shouted a warning.

Madame La Geness had scrabbled across the floor, her hand once more reaching for the whip.

Brodie pushed me aside and quickly moved past. He stood over her with a revolver in hand.

"Stop! Or you will wish she had crushed yer hand."

Sarah, with bruised and tear-stained face, quickly grabbed the whip as Madame glared up at Brodie.

"Best use that leather whip to bind her," he told Sarah.

I helped her, my anger at what this woman had done very near the surface as I tightened the leather bonds, not satisfied until she made a sound of protest.

"And bind her across the mouth. She can save her protests for the police." He jerked the tie from about his neck and handed it to the girl as I slowly stood.

Brodie was here.

I had no way of knowing how ... It didn't matter.

A warm hand slipped to mine, his fingers gently squeezed mine as I looked at him with that dark hair, those faint lines at the corners of that dark gaze, and several days' growth of beard.

"You found me," I whispered. More than that wasn't there yet.

"Aye, I found ye."

"It certainly took you long enough," I finally managed to add.

A smile lifted one corner of his mouth.

"I would have been here sooner, but yer notes lacked a bit of information. I had to pay Mr. Burke a visit."

Always one to have the last say.

"I can imagine how that went."

"Aye, I was forced to convince him to cooperate."

I would have laughed, aware that his opinion of the man was much like my own. But instead it sounded very much like someone struggling to breathe, as a sound came from the hallway, that familiar baying sound.

"Rupert?" I whispered through tears that I tried to wipe away.

The hound came charging through the doorway, followed by Munro as he dragged La Geness with him.

"The beast discovered this very near the wheelhouse," Munro explained, as if the man was a piece of trash that the hound had scrounged from the street. He dumped him on the floor.

"A bit the worse for wear, as the hound got to him first. But he'll give no trouble now."

"There's a stableman ..." I managed to tell him.

"I saw no one as I made my way to the gatehouse," Munro said, then glanced past us.

"Wot do we have here?" he asked with a look at the woman who sat on the floor, now firmly bound.

She tried to scream, no doubt with a curse for good

measure, but it was muffled beneath the cloth bound across her mouth.

Sarah slowly approached. "My name is Sarah Meeks. The others …"

"They're safe," I assured her.

"Thank you," she whispered amid a new flood of tears.

I was finally able to sleep after returning to the office, but not before a thorough scrubbing that included my hair in the loo down the hall, not to mention a bit of Old Lodge whisky and Brodie.

Gwen Tavers and Charlotte Davies along with Sarah and Jolie were safe. As for La Geness and his wife …

They were now in police custody to answer for the murder of Lizzie Smith and others that might yet be known.

And Brodie was here. His fingers lightly brushed the cut on my cheek after he brought the blankets up over the both of us.

"Ye will be the death of me, Mikaela Forsythe," he whispered, his lips warm as they brushed my forehead.

"It is your fault, of course," I replied somewhat hazily as the whisky slowly had its way with me.

"Of course, I was able to figure it all out by myself …"

"Aye. But it will not happen again. Ye have my word on it."

"Yes, dear," I replied as I drifted off.

Eighteen

LONDON, #204 THE STRAND

INSPECTOR DOOLEY ACCEPTED another cup of coffee as he sat across the desk from Brodie.

"We confiscated the paintings from the Grosvenor Gallery. And we have the statements made by the women. I doubt La Geness will be much help.

"He's been taken with spells that the physician has assured are real. It seems that the difficulty has been coming on for some time. He could barely walk when the lads brought him in. The portraits ..." he shook his head.

"It seems that his wife had painted them, though he was part of the scheme."

I thought of my first encounter at the Grosvenor, the trembling I had seen before he appeared to hide his hands from view. Afflicted with a sort of palsy that it appeared would have gradually taken his ability to paint.

"There'll not be any objections from anyone when I bring the case before the magistrate," Mr. Dooley added, without actually naming the person we all knew—Chief Inspector Abberline, recently reinstated after some time away.

He took a sip of coffee, frowned, then held the cup out.

"Ah, that is better. Soothes the spirit," he commented as Brodie set the bottle of Old Lodge back on the desk.

"I sent a telegram off to the Prefect of Police in Paris," he continued. "It seems there is more to this than what happened here. It seems that three young women who appeared in those portraits at the gallery have also been reported as missing."

It was a chilling outcome, yet I was reminded there was often no length some would go in protecting their crime.

"We also took the paintings from the manor at Knightsbridge as well, for evidence." He gave Brodie a long look.

"It seems there may be one missing."

I caught a look with Brodie. A missing painting? One that might have found its way to the office late the previous night, courtesy of Munro?

"And I will be the only one to see it," Brodie had announced at the time. "I'll not have others gaping at ye."

That, according to a man who had once claimed he had no cause to be jealous over any woman.

The painting was now propped against the wall in the bedroom where no one might see it. Except, of course, Munro, who had retrieved it, and the man I was married to.

I had thought the portrait quite flattering. Although the 'artist'—Madame La Geness, had missed the tattoo on the back of my right shoulder.

There had been a brief conversation about how the painting came to be, including the gown shown in the painting that resembled one that I had worn.

I had assured him that I had not posed for it.

"When might I have had time for that?" I pointed out.

I had also informed him that the gown was the same color as

the one I had worn to the Grosvenor Gallery with Linnie, that both La Geness and Madame La Geness had no doubt remembered, with that slight alteration of course. Easily copied, I reminded him.

There had been another colorful comment after that, and then, "I can see I canna let ye out of my sight."

The most important thing was that the young women were safe.

That included Gwen Tavers, who was first brought to my attention as missing. Mr. Cavendish had thanked me in that direct way of his, and I had received a note of gratitude from Reggie Tavers.

"I knew you would find her. My thanks, miss."

"The Davies girl comes from a well-placed family, with her father in the Home Office," Inspector Dooley now continued. "As for the other girls …"

Both Gwen Tavers and Charlotte Davies had returned to their families. Sarah had worked in her family's bakery shop and had answered that advertisement the same as the others, with the hope for travel and adventure beyond scones, cakes, and loaves of bread.

As we had left Knightsbridge the night before, she wanted only to see them again.

"What of Jolie?" I inquired. I had not seen any of the other young women after they left the gate house and had eventually found a driver who took them to the Bond Street Station where Mr. Dooley was contacted.

"The Davies family has insisted that she's to stay with them for now. She doesn't want to return to Paris. Understandable, with everything that has happened."

"My great-aunt might be able to help," I suggested.

I would speak with her when there was more time than the

brief telephone conversation Brodie had made the night before to reassure her that I was safe.

"What will happen to Monsieur La Geness and his wife?" I asked.

"Murder charges to be certain in the death of Lizzie Smith, and additional charges in the abduction and imprisonment of the others," Mr. Dooley replied.

"Further charges are usually left to the magistrate," Brodie explained. "And there is the matter of your imprisonment as well," he added.

Mr. Dooley nodded. "The man apparently had no part in the Smith girl's murder. He can barely hold a cup for the shaking in his hands, let alone paint those portraits.

"Though he had his own part in the planning of it, putting the portraits on display, and accepting some sort of arrangement to tour with them. That will be for the courts to determine as well. It seems that it was the woman who beat the Smith girl senseless, and then had the man Brodie encountered take her off to get rid of her. Poor thing."

He stood to leave.

"There should be some reward in this for the hound," he suggested, with a shake of his head.

"Strange as it is, it makes sense—a hound that can find people."

"He seems to have a preference for one person in particular," Brodie replied.

It undoubtedly had something to do with the biscuits I provided Rupert. And he did have a preference for Mrs. Ryan's sponge cake.

"I need for you to come to Bond Street, to make your statement," Mr. Dooley reminded me. He paused.

"The La Geness woman kept goin' on about how you

threatened her? Said she was afraid for her life. It seems she did receive an injury to her wrist and hand."

"I have no idea what she might be talking about."

Brodie said nothing, however I did catch the look he gave me.

"All well and good," Inspector Dooley replied. "Still, it was a dangerous thing, goin' off on yer own."

Brodie agreed with a look at me. "We'll be havin' a conversation about that."

After Mr. Dooley left, I went to the chalkboard and slowly wiped it clean. I had my notebook back and would provide a report to Mr. Dooley from notes I had made.

Then there was the matter of Brodie's visit to Theodolphus Burke for information on those advertisements that had posted on the Personals page of The Times.

That is a meeting I would very much like to have witnessed.

He came up behind me, and that the scent of cinnamon was there.

"Ye should have taken the hound with ye."

"I did think about it, however in the moment it seemed that he might cause suspicion and endanger the women, since I had no way of knowing where they were."

"And ye didna consider that yer bein' there might cause suspicion?" he pointed out.

"It was important to act quickly on the information I had, as I recall *someone* once telling me about investigations, particularly where lives might be in danger, and ..." I paused.

He turned me about and pulled me close. A familiar tactic when he was determined to make a point. Not that I objected.

"We need to re-examine our working relationship, Mikaela Forsythe."

"And that might be?"

"Ye are not to take yerself off alone again as ye did. I'll not have her ladyship to answer to ..."

He paused, his expression softening. "Ye are a troublesome baggage, Mikaela Forsythe Brodie."

Such an endearing sentiment, but I would take it.

"Do tell me about your work for the Agency, now that it is concluded. Was there something Aunt Antonia said that proved useful?" I pointedly inquired.

"The information about the Blandfords was critical in being able to ... resolve the matter," he admitted, without sharing more.

"You might have concluded it earlier, if you had included me in *your* inquiries from the beginning," I pointed out. "And then you might have accompanied me in my inquiry case."

He brushed my cheek with his fingers with a frown that deepened.

It was difficult from time to time, to accept that I was right about something—that stubborn Scots nature.

"Merely pointing out the facts, Mr. Brodie."

"Point taken."

He brushed a kiss at the cut on my cheek.

"When I saw the blood and the bruises ..."

Some women might want words of endearment, yet I sensed them in the way his voice lowered to barely more than a whisper.

"An accident, when I was attempting to free myself. Which might not have been necessary ..."

"As I said, troublesome," he kissed me again. "But I wouldna want to have to train someone else to take yer place, if anything happened to ye."

"Train someone?"

When I would have objected further, he pressed his fingers against my lips.

"I will not be takin' work again with the Agency," he continued. "I am through with that, particularly anything that would prevent me being here. Ye have my word on it. We'll make it work, though cases, as ye know, can be few and far between, and there are expenses."

"You seem to forget, Mr. Brodie, that I am a woman of some means. With my trust money, book royalties, and the townhouse in Mayfair, we shall carry on."

"I'll not live off yer money. I've told ye that before," he reminded me, a somewhat heated discussion in the past.

"But it seems that the matter of the office rents has been taken care of," he added.

"In a matter of speaking."

I frowned. "How might that be?"

He reached around me and retrieved a thick envelope that I remembered from days earlier at the edge of his desk.

"It would seem that her ladyship has taken matters into her own hands in that regard." He handed me the envelope.

I retrieved the papers from inside the envelope. The first was a letter of explanation for a document that had been enclosed, which I immediately turned to.

It was a Deed of Conveyance from the Chelmsford Investment Company for property known in official records as #104 and #204 Strand, London, United Kingdom, with the legal description, previously known as block number and appurtenant building, as of 14 May 1893.

And so on and such, with the name of the owner given, A. W. Brodie of #204 Strand, London.

There was also a note attached from my aunt's attorney, Sir Laughton:

"Her ladyship insisted upon this, along with her fondness and good wishes for you both."

"So it would seem that the rents are taken care of," I commented, as I folded the papers and returned them to the envelope.

"You are not put off about it? Yer great-aunt giving me title to the property?"

"Not at all," I replied. "Although as your wife, I am entitled to inherit any property you have, should you succumb to some injury.

"Not to mention, that someday, which I hope is very far away, my sister and I will inherit Sussex Square and all of Aunt Antonia's holdings. You have married quite well, sir."

"I did not marry ye for such things," he reminded me.

"Why did you ask me to marry you?" I inquired, as the precise reason had never been explained.

"Ye are intelligent, bold, and more brave than ye should be. Not to mention that ye have a keen mind when it comes to solving a crime, even tho' ye land yerself in the middle of dangerous situations."

I had heard that before.

At present I chose not to remind him that he had very nearly arrived too late in Knightsbridge. I would save that for later, although I would very definitely have broken the woman's neck, if he had not arrived when he did.

"And?" I prompted him, since he was sharing his deepest and innermost thoughts.

"It was the way ye looked when I found you on that beach on the island of Crete, as if ye would defy the devil himself, with yer hair down about yer shoulders and the look ye gave me."

And a confession.

"I wanted ye then and no other, even if it meant I might never see ye again after I brought ye back to London."

"Wanted me?"

"I shoulda known better, you bein' a lady, and meself from the streets."

"But now, a man of property," I reminded him. "I suppose that shall have to do."

"There is another matter we must discuss," he added.

"And what might that be?" I replied.

He reached into the pocket of his trousers, then opened his hand.

"You misplaced this."

"My ring! I thought it was gone forever!"

When I reached for it, he held it just beyond my reach.

"Mr. Dooley learned of it from the women and was able to retrieve it from the driver who took them to the Bond Street Station. Ye are not only a troublesome baggage, but a careless one as well."

"It was all I had of value after my travel bag was taken," I explained. "And I was determined that the women would leave that place. You would have done the same," I pointed out.

"Determined. Aye, ye are that Mikaela Forsythe Brodie, and more." He held it between his fingers. "I would buy you another with a stone. Now that I'm a man of property."

I finally managed to take it from him and slipped it onto my finger, with that saying in Gaelic that he'd had engraved on the inside.

An-còmhnaidh. Always.

Quite sentimental for a man who claimed he was not the least sentimental about anything.

It fit perfectly.

Preview… Deadly Murder

BOOK 14, ANGUS BRODIE AND MIKAELA FORSYTHE MURDER MYSTERY

WE WAITED in the drawing room of the suite at the Grand Hotel after receiving what might be called a royal summons, on plain note paper, signed simply E. A, and with a cryptic message that we meet.

I was familiar with those initials that I had seen at the conclusion of our first inquiry case. E.A., Edward Albert the Prince of Wales.

'*We*', referred to both Brodie and myself according to an agreement that neither of us would undertake *separate* cases after a particular situation that could have ended badly. Although I did have it well in hand by the time he arrived.

After that prior situation, there had been the odd case or two, both quite minor, with most of our time devoted to the changes we wanted to make at the office, now that Brodie was the official owner of the building on the Strand.

Such as the lift we were having installed to assist those for whom the stairs presented an obstacle. I originally thought of Mr. Cavendish, who assisted us from time to time in our inquiries, while Brodie had pointed out that it might be convenient for my great-aunt, who made frequent visits when she was out and about in her motor carriage.

The lift was to be powered by electricity and was very nearly completed, along with an expansion of the loo upstairs, repairs to the ground floor shop at #104 that had stood empty, and then a remodel project of third floor.

Brodie was determined to let out the ground floor shop to a business prospect. He was, after all, a Scot and determined that ownership of the building should include rental income. The third floor which had been vacant for some time needed a great amount of work. My great-aunt had ideas about that. I could only imagine what that might include.

He had left Mr. Cavendish in charge of the final test for the lift after the arrival of the 'unofficial' summons, delivered by one of the courier services about London rather than by official royal courier. Most intriguing.

So here we were, awaiting the arrival of his Royal Highness.

I was familiar with the suite of rooms at the Grand as I had been there before with my good friend, Templeton, who, at the time, was rumored to be the *theatre companion* of the Prince of Wales.

That particular title was subject to interpretations—mistress, and lover being two of them, although she had vehemently denied it.

'We are just very good friends.'

Good friends, my foot!

However, I did like Templeton very much, a well-travelled, independent woman much like myself. We got along without any pretenses and shared a good joke or two from time to time. And she was forever attempting to persuade me to join her on her next tour to the United States. However, that had been pre-empted by the man who presently paced the floor of the suite.

"How am I supposed to greet the man?" Brodie asked with a frown. "I canna exactly slap him on the back and offer to buy him a pint," he said with more than a little sarcasm.

"Aside from the slap on the back, you might simply say— 'Good afternoon,'" I suggested as I stood and straightened his tie. "And then let him provide the reason for the meeting."

Their past acquaintance had been cordial without the usual formalities required when speaking to a royal. Yet, that might have had to do with the fact that Brodie had just saved the man's life and those of his family.

"He signed the note with only the initials, E.A." he commented.

"Obviously to put the situation at ease," I explained.

As well as for secrecy? And then sending it by common courier. Most unusual.

Now, we awaited when he might appear and provide information regarding the situation. Although, considering past rumored transgressions, affairs, several mistresses in addition to my friend, I could only imagine the need for that discretion.

"But what reason for the plain message, and no royal courier?" Brodie commented.

The question was rhetorical, in that way that we often traded questions, thoughts, suggestions when on an inquiry case.

It was then that I heard the door to the suite open, and His Royal Highness, Edward Albert, the Prince of Wales and future King of England, entered the room.

"It seems that we are about to learn the reason."

The Prince of Wales was dressed informally in a trousers and jacket of the finest quality but that might have been worn for a day out sporting or at his hunting lodge. A cap in one hand, his other was extended to Brodie in greeting.

No personal staff accompanied him: no equerry, nor Sir Knollys, his private secretary. Not even a footman.

"I appreciate your meeting with me at such short notice, Mr. Brodie," the Prince of Wales greeted him.

"Good afternoon, sir."

His Highness turned to me. "And Lady Forsythe. Always a pleasure."

I smothered back a smile at Brodie's frown at the mention of pleasure and made a formal acknowledgement.

"No formalities, please," he said then.

Another insight into what was obviously a very serious matter.

"Shall we begin?" Brodie replied, with a gesture to the over-stuffed settee and two side chairs that sat before the fireplace.

His highness nodded and then sat at the settee. Brodie and I each took a chair across from him.

"I have not forgotten your service in the past on behalf of myself and my family, Mr. Brodie and Lady Forsythe.

"It is in that regard that I sent that note. There is a matter that has arisen that is somewhat alarming and of a nature that could be most serious for my family." He seemed genuinely disturbed as he continued.

"I assure you that it is not what you might assume from past rumors about certain indiscretions."

It was the only reference he made to several well-known affairs which I was aware of, and which my great-aunt had known of from years past. The man did have a fondness not only for actresses, but a titled lady or two of my great-aunt's acquaintance.

"It seems as though the man cannot keep his trousers buttoned," she had remarked when one particular affair became

known. *"And then there was that nonsense about a chair or some other piece of furniture."*

I did appreciate that she hadn't shared details on that particular subject.

"I much prefer a rogue to a nobleman," she had continued at the time. *"It does add excitement, wouldn't you agree, dear?"*

I looked over at Brodie. I had to admit that I did agree on that.

The 'rogue', or the Scot, was presently dressed much like a gentleman, his expression thoughtful, his deportment flawless so that one might almost think him a gentleman. Almost.

His Highness stood then and paced across the room.

"I must ask for your discretion and secrecy, of course, until the purpose behind this is determined."

Brodie nodded. "Of course."

I nodded as well, although we had yet to learn what the situation might be.

His Highness reached inside his jacket and retrieved an envelope. He removed a folded piece of stationary and handed it to Brodie.

"I received this late last evening."

Brodie unfolded the stationary read the contents, then handed it to me.

I read the note, then looked up.

"The sins of the father will be visited upon the children ... "

Author Notes

It often seems that the more things change ... the more they stay the same.

And that is true with frightening consequences when three women disappear, to be used for one person's maniacal scheme.

Deadly Attraction provided the opportunity to speak out about things that seem to transcend time and place, particularly the exploitation of women.

Unfortunately, history does repeat itself. And Mikaela is not only a very modern, independent woman for her time, but a staunch defender of those who cannot defend themselves.

As for other elements of Brodie and Mikaela's latest investigation—yes, Brodie did finally make an appearance, the timing for reasons that were necessary, and she was very prompt in pointing out that he was late!

I assure you that will change going forward, but an element to emphasize that they are far better together than separate. And there is that other part of it. Something about one's toes ...!

The end of the 19th century is rapidly approaching for Brodie and Mikaela, with more innovations, challenges, and dangers.

Electric overhead fans were prominent in shops and upper-class residences, first as a large set of paddles that tumbled one over one another on a frame, then later as the 'fan-like' mechanism that we know today. Things that have stayed the same.

And along that same thought: The Times of London did publish a Personals advertisement page—page one of the daily, that promoted proposals of marriage and other 'arrangements,' not unlike modern texting, email messages for hook-ups and dating sites.

An even earlier publication than the one I've used was referred to as the Lonely Hearts publication around 1860. And of course, in the United States after the Civil War, there were publications that advertised for brides and 'companions' if the person was willing to travel West, train fare provided.

Posters were often placed about London for travel adventures, along with postcards of places for those longing to leave behind the dreariness and the brown haze and fog of London. Formal tours were offered by Thomas Cook and Son.

Harrod's Department Store in London was originally established in 1849 as a grocery shop. It went through several changes, including its transformation into an upscale department store that burned down in 1883, was then rebuilt, and reopened in 1905, and is what people find today in London.

There are several Punch taverns throughout the UK, originally established in 1840's London.

Knightsbridge was originally a very rural village, with large tracts of farmland and large manors of wealthy landowners. As London grew and expanded in the 18th and 19th centuries, the rural countryside gave way to row houses, townhouses, and establishments such as Harrod's and other fashionable shops and hotels. Including the fashionable Sloane Square. Ah, progress.

The Deed of Conveyance that provides title for #104 and #204 the Strand to Brodie as a gift from Aunt Antonia was carefully researched. The Act of 1882 that was passed by Parliament finally allowed married women to hold property in their own names.

Of course, this would have applied mostly to women of the middle and upper classes. As for the office at #204, Mikaela obviously was not concerned that her name was not listed on the title. As she pointed out, she would inherit the office building when Brodie passed on (which is not anticipated).

Another small bit of information, the knife that Mikaela carries which I referred to as a switch knife (or switch blade), was actually first invented as a folding spike bayonet for use on flintlock pistols and coach guns as early as 1742. The version that I have used in the story was perfected by a clockmaker in Sheffield, England, and carries a Crown marking.

As for Brodie's promise that they will not work separately again, do read on for a preview of DEADLY MURDER, Book 14.

Angus Brodie and Mikaela Forsythe Murder Mystery

A Deadly Affair

Deadly Secrets

A Deadly Game

Deadly Illusion

A Deadly Vow

Deadly Obsession

A Deadly Deception

A Deadly Betrayal

A Deadly Scandal

Deadly Lies

Deadly Curse

Deadly Ghost

Deadly Attraction

Merlin Series

Daughter of Fire

Daughter of the Mist

Daughter of the Light

Shadows of Camelot

Dawn of Camelot

Daughter of Camelot

The Young Dragons, Blood Moon

Clan Fraser

Betrayed

Revenge

Outlaws, Scoundrels & Lawmen

Desperado's Caress

Passion's Splendor

Silver Mistress

Memory and Desire

Desire's Flame

Silken Surrender

Angels, Devils, Rebels & Rogues

Ravished

Always My Love

Seductive Caress

Seduced

Deceived

About the Author

"I want to write a book ..." she said.

"Then do it," he said.

And she did, and received two offers for that first book proposal.

A dozen historical romances later, and a prophecy from a gifted psychic and the Legacy Series was created, expanding to seven additional titles.

Along the way, two film options, and numerous book awards.

But wait, there's more a voice whispered, after a trip to Scotland and a visit to the standing stones in the far north, and as old as Stonehenge, sign posts the voice told her, and the Clan Fraser books that have followed that told the beginnings of the clan and the family she was part of ...

And now ... murder and mystery set against the backdrop of Victorian London in the new Angus Brodie and Mikaela Forsythe series, with an assortment of conspirators and murderers in the brave new world after the Industrial Revolution where terrorists threaten and the world spins closer to war.

When she is not exploring the Darkness of the fantasy world, or pursuing ancestors in ancient Scotland, she lives in the mountains near Yosemite National Park with bears and mountain lions, and plots murder and revenge.

And did I mention fierce, beautiful women and dangerous, handsome men?

They're there, waiting ...

Join Carla's Newsletter